CASTLES & CAULDRONS
A CASTLE POINT WITCH SERIES
BOOK TWO

TAMMY TYREE

Shale Empire Press

TAMMY TYREE

CASTLES
AND
CAULDRONS

A CASTLE POINT WITCH SERIES
BOOK 2

ISBN: Large Print 9798223155409

ISBN: Paperback 9781738979226

ISBN: (Ebook) 9781738979233

Any references to historical events, real people, or real places are used fictitiously. Names, characters, and places are products of the author's imagination.

Front cover image by Mibl Art

Book designed with Vellum

First printing edition 2023

Shale Empire Press

shaleempire@gmail.com

www.tammytyreebooks.com

For Jen
Whose demons were far too real
You are missed

ACKNOWLEDGMENTS

Huge thanks to my admin (and daughter), Chloe, for her hard work and tenacity in learning allllll the things about the world of Indie Publishing.

Thanks to Carissa, Camilla, and Christine (The 3 C's) for your friendship, support, encouragement, and being the best cheering squad I know!

Many thanks to my Alpha-reader, Kaitlin, and my amazing ARC team for their input and feedback. You guys ROCK!

Also, to my newsletter subscribers for their continued engagement and support.

AUTHOR'S NOTE

This is a work of fiction.
The story of Madeline Bavant and the demon Dagon is real.

Mostly...

PROLOGUE

T he History of Madeline Bavant & Earl Dagon

In 1647, a convent chapel in Louviers, France was struck by a mass demonic possession. Sister Madeline Bavant prompted the possession of eighteen nuns who, according to her confession, were believed to be under the spell of Mathurin Picard, the former — and deceased — director of the nunnery, and Father Thomas Boulle, the vicar at Louviers.

Bavent asserted that Picard's bewitchment from 'beyond the grave' was causing the nuns to become possessed. She further attributed this to certain dubious spiritual practices that had been linked to the convent.

Bavent disclosed to authorities that the two clergymen had taken her to a witch's Sabbat, where she met and wedded the demon, Earl Dagon, and committed grotesque and indecent acts with him on the altar.

In response, the bishop of Evreaux ordered for Picard's body to be exhumed and destroyed, in an attempt to stop the possessions.

But, Madeline Bavent had lied.

It wasn't the deceased Picard or Father Boulle who were responsible for the demonic possession, it was Madeline herself, under the spell of the evil Earl.

Subsequently, the Earl brought his new bride, Madeline, to Castle Point, where they established their bloodline.

I am the last surviving descendant of their evil blood.

Not my best trait.

And it gets worse...

You'll just have to keep reading to find out...

ALEXANDRA HEALE.

CHAPTER
ONE

ALEXANDRA

E arl Dagon was chasing me.
        I couldn't see his face, but I could hear him. His heavy footsteps were closing in on me. My breath quickened as I slipped in and out of the dark corners of Castle Dagon, desperately trying to find a place to hide. I could almost feel his breath, hot and putrid, as he huffed and puffed with the pace of his footsteps. His voice, a fleeting thought..

"You can't hide from me, Evelyn. I know you're here. I will find you, my darling. You will be mine again."

I opened my mouth to scream "No!" but nothing came. Chilly spikes of fear stabbed every part of me. I lunged forward, into another dark corner, heading toward the castle door. The Earl, hearing me, quickly shifted and closed in on me once again.

Every step I took felt like running through sludge. My feet, heavy with fear and tired from running, threatened to fail me before reaching the door. With all my energy, I took the last lunge towards the door. Pulling back, like a cat about to pounce, *with heavy legs leaped forward, willing the voluminous sludge to release my feet. I lunged for the door.*

Earl Dagon snarled, his footsteps right behind me. A large, clammy hand clasped around my neck, forcing me back, then spinning me around, toppling me to the ground...

I woke up when I hit the floor.

Relief flooded my body as I looked around, recognizing my bedroom. I was wrapped in a burrito of blankets and sheets, laying on the floor. Sticky sweat dampened the sheets and my hair, now clinging to my face and wrapped around my neck...like a large hand, choking me.

It was a dream. A really terrible, terrible dream.

They were coming more frequently now, since my daring jaunt to Castle Dragon to get a peek at an ancient book sequestered under lock and key in the library. Blackjack and I had taken a wee nap in an off—tour bedroom, waiting for everyone to skedaddle. I had my first dream of the Earl then. He seemed to mistake me for his Evelyn of Cumbria—the witch he professed to love, who broke his heart and ended up burning on the castle pyre.

The Earl Dagon wasn't after me. He wasn't even alive. He was a piece of my history, my ancestry long since dead.

Thank the Goddess.

Blackjack sauntered into the room as I attempted to free my arms from their tangled position. He jumped up on my chest and sat.

"Havin' some troubles, woman?" His silky voice floated through my mind.

"A bad dream, Blackjack."

Blackjack lay where he sat, curling his paws under his chest. *"I heard a thump. Did you fall off the bed? Or have you taken to sleeping on the floor?"*

I peered at him, my arms still trapped in the blankets,

gobs of hair masking my face. "I fell off the bed, you goober."

"Oh, what fun." Blackjack's emerald green eyes, a match to my own, glistened. *"You should probably get off the dusty floor. You're not the best housekeeper, you know. Your dust bunnies have dust bunnies,"* he pulled out a paw and licked it.

"Ever so helpful, as always, you mangy brat." He was far from mangy, but I knew what 'piss-him-off' buttons to push. His fur, also a match to my hair, a luxurious jet—black from hours of incessant cleaning, shone in the sun now beating through my bedroom window.

I rolled, tossing a surprised cat onto the floor. His legs splayed out, momentarily gripping the blankets before he recovered and sat, casually licking the same paw he'd been busy with a moment earlier.

Blackjack stopped licking long enough to stare up at me as I shook the sheets from my body and stood. *"You're pre-caffeine personality leaves much to be desired."*

"Back at ya you little demon." I gathered the blankets, tore the fitted sheet from the bed, and piled them on the floor in the hall to put in the laundry after my shower. Blackjack strutted from the room, tail high in the air. For a twenty—something cat with attitude, I couldn't imagine living a day without him. Luckily, I wouldn't have to. He was a gift from my mentor, Waldo Cress, before 'Cressy' continued his mentoring from the other side. Blackjack was a kitten when Cressy gave him to me. A magical familiar that was bound to be mine until the day we both crossed over and joined Cressy on the other side.

In the meantime, I had to put up with his snobbery and blasphemous back end.

I mean, the farts that cat could conjure...

A giggle—snort escaped my lips just thinking about it.

I didn't really mind. Other than a handful of friends, I had no other relationship in my life, so Blackjack filled the cuddling void—when he was in the mood. He was family, in the absence of my own. Well, not a complete absence. My mother was still alive but sequestered in a mental institution one county over, suffering from a severe case of Demon's Curse. One I've never been able to solve. I got further along in that quest when my best friend Penny helped me a few short weeks ago. Mom sort of came out of her 'stupor' for a bit and started writing—some ancient text that I have no translation of. But I had seen the text earlier, both from a spirit I was trying to help and from an ancient, very large book in Castle Dagon, now a museum and shrine to the late and not—so—great (at least to me) Earl Dagon.

I shuddered, my earlier dream sifting through my mind as I got out of the shower, dressed, and headed downstairs to launder my sheets and concoct my morning ritual; Caramel Macchiato. Blackjack was waiting by his dish when I stepped into the kitchen.

"Jeez, woman. What took so long? I've been hovering over my dish for hours.*"*

"Ok, Mr. Over-exaggerator. If you want food faster, grow some opposable thumbs and open the can yourself." I pulled the easy top off the tin of cat food and shook it over Blackjack's dish. It landed with a wet plop. Blackjack sniffed, then delicately licked the fishy goop.

"You're welcome."

"Mm—hmm. Good human."

I finished creating my macchiato to perfection and took a sip, dismantling the wacky coffee foam art as I did so. Today I attempted a tree. It looked more like a blobby stick with a couple of branches, but it was better than the usual genitalia that had recently become my specialty since I gave up trying to pour a simple heart.

I checked my phone. My best friend and psychic witch Penny, and Teddy, my apothecary shopkeeper, group texted me. We made a date to meet in the back room of the apothecary later today, to plan for Samhain, the Feast of the Dead, which also happened to be my birthday. Also, there were packages of ritual herbs and potions to create and send out to the underground witch population of Dagon County, so witches everywhere could celebrate as they always had; in solitude.

Although we had only recently formed a coven, celebrating in large groups was definitely not on the agenda. Calling attention to a group of witches while living in a world where witchcraft was illegal was definitely a ludicrous idea.

One that would certainly end with us burning on the Castle Dagon pyre.

We could thank Earl Dagon for that honor.

The bane of a witch's existence, not just in Dagon County, but beyond. His 400-year-old law against the practice of witchcraft spread to the far reaches of the earth, thanks to the Order of the Witch Hunters, devout followers of Earl Dagon, and his Dark Lord; the Demon Vine.

Spreading the hate and belief that witches are pure evil was Earl Dagon's legacy.

One I'm ashamed to be part of. As one of the last of the Earl's unfiltered lineage, his blood runs through my veins.

Hence the no relationship part.

I didn't need to pass that legacy on, no way.

A self-imposed do-gooder, I preferred my witchy side.

If only there was a way to tear down the law and end

the Witch Hunter's reign, then witches would be free to practice and meet and celebrate together.

Kind of like what Penny, Teddy, and I were doing for Samhain.

We planned to celebrate—just the three of us—in the privacy of the back room of the apothecary. That wouldn't raise any alarm bells should the non-mage population of Castle Point see Penny, Teddy, and me together. Just three friends, hanging out in my shop.

No big deal.

Nothing to see here, folks. Go about your business and stay out of mine.

I clung to that wish as I tossed back the last of my macchiato and got ready to leave.

CHAPTER
TWO

ALEXANDRA

The town of Castle Point was its usual Sunday quiet. I savored the peace as I walked from my home on Ocean View Drive, into town a few short blocks away, Blackjack running in spurts beside me. The crisp autumn air sent a pleasing chill through me, but I zipped my jacket a little higher, stuffing my hands into the pockets.

I nodded at the few people I passed on the way and received their 'hello's' and 'good days' gratefully. Many people in the community were clients of either my apothecary or my therapy practice.

None of them knew I was a witch.

Except one.

Chief Deputy Blake Sheraton.

The hot, dreamy Sheriff had a list of flaws that could circle the sun. His looks were not one of them. Just thinking about Blake's biceps caused gooseflesh to break out all over my body—including my nips. Pointy nip bumps rubbed the inside of my bra. Damn that man. I hadn't seen him in days, ignoring his calls after he attempted to kiss me. I needed time to slough off the titillating craving my disobedient body had for the man. Getting involved with a cop sworn to uphold the law, especially ancient laws against witchcraft and witches, was definitely not a great idea. Thinking of him clearly spurned a jolt of heat through my uncooperative body.

Although he had promised not to turn me in after using my witchy abilities to save him from a demon attack, I still didn't feel like I could trust him. Then, when he made a move on me, I pushed him away. Because, how could I be attracted to a man who did—and could—make my life a living hell?

He was the high school football all-star athlete, but he was also my tormentor in high school. Pretty sure I saw the inside of my locker more than I did my classes. Blake had recently apologized for being such a big meanie, but I still held a cautious grudge. His relentless torment caused my evil Dagon blood to boil one fateful Friday afternoon, resulting in a shredded high school, an injured football team, a long-term forgetting spell, and a stint in Juvie.

For me, that is.

Thanks to a fast-thinking Cressy and his powerful spell over the principal and students, my fate could have been so much worse.

Burning on the pyre in Castle Dagon.

I mean, how much worse could it get?

I reached the Castle Point Apothecary—a shop handed down to me by Cressy himself—and unlocked the front door. Penny and Teddy were already inside. Today being Sunday, there was little in the way of open shops, mine included. The exception was a couple of small diners, both in town and on the seaside.

The front of the shop was stark white, shelves filled with handmade bath products either Teddy, me, or other artisans produced. Penny was busy unscrewing the tops of bottles and taking a deep sniff.

"Good Goddess, that smells divine." She screwed the cap back onto one bottle before snatching another and repeating the process, leaned over, and drew a deep breath. Her long, curly red hair fell around her curvy body.

Teddy giggled, her multicolored pigtails shaking. "Buy before you try, lady. Howdy Doody Alex!"

"Hi, Teddy. Nice Tat!" Teddy's knowledge of the craft started with Glamor 101. A simple talent she mastered almost immediately, and one she used to 'glamor', a change to her hair, makeup, and tattoos almost daily. They—and her colorful use of the English language—added a dash of delight to her black clothing palette. Today's choice depicted a whale chasing a porpoise, chasing a penguin. "Got a little ocean theme going, I see."

Teddy looked at her arms. "Yessiree-bob, I watched a whale breach earlier today when I took the hell hounds for walkies up to the castle."

"You did what now?" Penny paused, mid sniff at Teddy's mention of Castle Dagon.

"The best views of the ocean are up there on the point," Teddy explained. She wasn't wrong. The Castle sat on the highest point—hence the name of the town, Castle Point. Views of the ocean, the town below, and beyond, were absolutely stunning.

Too bad it was the birthplace of great evil.

Gosh darn it.

"Just be careful you don't work on any spells or glamors outside your own home or the back room of the shop, Teddy," I warned. "I mean, you're already taking a chance by changing your glamor tattoos and hair. If anyone noticed a daily difference, you could be in deep kaka." Teddy was a little new to Castle Point and the witch game. I was happy to be her mentor and felt responsible for her. A job I didn't take lightly.

Teddy nodded. "I know, I know. I'm careful—pinky-swear promise." She stuck out her pinky, encircling mine for a quick shake. "I always revert to the same-old same-old before work every day, boss lady." I smiled and gave her a quick hug before shuttling the gals to the back room of the shop.

A stark opposite the front of the shop, the dark wood floor, walls, and shelves in my secret witchy storeroom smelled of rich, earthy herbs. Penny stood in the center of the room, arms outstretched, head back, and took a deep, long breath. "Ahhhh, it just smells so amazing."

My lips curved into a wide smile. "You're all about the smells today, hey Pen?"

"Just taking it all in. Life, that is. It's so wonderful, isn't it? I mean—we're *alive*." She grabbed my shoulders and pulled me in for a tight squeeze. My breath left my body and refused to return.

"Pen, what's got into you?" I huffed out, using the last remaining air in my lungs.

She released me, holding my shoulders. "I'm just happy to be alive, is all."

I quirked a brow. "Sure, Pen. Being alive is great."

She bobbed her head in agreement, red curls floating around her shoulders, before releasing me and reaching for Teddy. Teddy squeaked and ran to the other side of the desk in the center of the room. "You'll crush me!"

Penny, arms still outstretched, swung over to Teddy's hell hounds instead. Glamored as Bull Mastiffs', the hounds gratefully accepted Penny's love. "Who's a good Lucius, huh? Who's a good Draco? Who's a good boy," she purred before getting on the ground and laying between the hounds, who cheerily lapped at her face and arms.

I could understand Penny's excitement at being on the top side of the soil. Or the not—burned side of the pyre. She had a scare a while back when she thought Blake found out she was a witch. I convinced him otherwise.

At least, I think I did.

Neither Penny nor I were on the pyre, so I guess it worked.

For now, anyway.

A tiny chill ran through me, coiling the muscles in my belly.

Shaking it off, I turned to the gals. Penny was still rolling around on the floor with the hounds. Teddy was sitting on top of the desk, watching and laughing.

A warmth spread through me, coating the previous chill.

"Well, ladies, shall we get the party plans started?"

THREE

ALEXANDRA

A fter a fun evening of planning, laughing, and a wee bit too much wine, I woke to the sun streaming through my bedroom window, hitting me squarely in the eyes.

No dreams, thank the Goddess.

Perhaps copious amounts of wine were the key. I could get on board with that if it meant not being chased in my dreams.

Blackjack sauntered into the room. *"Stayed off the floor last night, I see,"* he pounced onto my chest, taking up his usual morning seat.

I stroked his head. "No dreams last night Blackjack. All is good in my world."

"You say that now, but just wait until you see what's waiting for you outside."

I stopped, mid-stroke. "What you talkin' 'bout kitty?" He hated the moniker and narrowed his eyes at me. "Did someone break the protection jars again?" Hairs rose on my arms and back of my neck as I propped myself up on my elbows, staring up at Blackjack. My jars had been uprooted and broken only a few weeks ago. I still had no clue who the culprit was, but it definitely wasn't an animal.

Well, perhaps an animal of the demon variety.

I made a mental note to have security cameras installed. It was one of about twenty mental notes I'd made in that regard since the jars were first broken, but few of them made it to actual note paper.

"Yes. And as a bonus, someone thought it would be fun to decorate the trees with Poopy Paper."

"What?" I bolted up and out of bed, tossing Blackjack onto the floor. Taking huge strides to the window, I could see the trees surrounding my large, unfenced yard. They were covered in reams and reams of white toilet paper, fluttering mindlessly in the breeze. "What the actual crap?" I looked over at Blackjack, who was turning in circles on the unmade bed, prepping to lie down for his first nap of the day.

"Good pun, woman. Well done. Also, I don't know," he snuggled into the blankets.

I glared at him, hands on my hips. "You're a big help. Didn't hear anyone? See anything?"

Blackjack lifted his head long enough to give me a long look. *"Yes, I know. Nope, and Nope."*

Shaking my head, I pulled on some jeans, a sweater, and socks, yanking them on as I navigated the stairs and out the front door.

The large oak trees, currently void of leaves in their pre-winter phase, were covered in a coat of white toilet paper. I walked around the perimeter of the large, stark white Victorian home I grew up in. A blanket of t.p. was swathed over every tree and shrub around the house. On the four corners of the yard, my protection jars had been dug up, the glass smashed, the contents now a whisper on the breeze.

Just beyond the backyard, the ocean churned against the rocky cliffs in the early morning tide. The sea air blew the paper, bellowing in and out, as if the trees were drawing breath, then blowing out again. They were so well wrapped, however, that nothing floated away. The chill of the ocean air smacked my face, jolting me from a pre-caffeine slump. A shiver rushed through me. I grabbed at the tiny vial of Cressy's ashes dangling from my earring and gently tugged.

Who did this?

My first instinct was to use magic to free the trees of their paper bonds, but thought better of it. It was early, but not that early. Several of my neighbors would be up and about, so using magic out in the open would be too risky.

Besides, I should really report the vandalism.

Which meant calling Blake.

I rushed inside and retrieved my cell phone. Mammoth butterflies swooshed through my belly with each ring. I tugged on my tiny vial earring with my free hand.

Blake answered a little too jovially. "Alex! An early morning call? You are; either about to ask me over for foamy genitalia coffee or something is up."

My small smile threatened to crease the corners of my mouth. I'd been avoiding his calls lately, so I was kind of grateful he was in a good mood. "Hey, Blake. I actually need you…"

"Another demon to vanquish? I'm your guy."

"Ha. No, thankfully. Actually, something happened at my place…"

"I'll be right over." the line went dead. I stared at the phone for a moment, then dashed up the stairs to brush my hair and put on some makeup. Blackjack was fast asleep on the bed, a sputter of farts escaping his back end. He snored on despite the ruckus I was making rushing around the bedroom.

Familiar, he had down. As a watch-cat, he completely sucked.

"Don't worry about a thing, Blackjack, I've got this." My teasing fell on deaf sleepy kitty ears.

The doorbell rang. Good Goddess, he was fast. Was he watching my place? A cool shiver tickled the hairs on the back of my neck. Was he responsible for the broken jars and the t.p.?

I brushed off the idea as I skidded down the stairs, gripping the railing to keep from falling on my rump.

It didn't work.

Feet slipping out from under me, I took the last four steps on my ass. I straightened up, smoothing my hair and sweater before opening the door. The glorious scent of Blakes's Brut cologne and lavender mint shampoo—my personal creation sold in my shop—hit me with the fall breeze and I breathed it in. My knees quivered.

"Hey, Blake. Thanks for coming over so quickly. You must have been in the neighborhood."

Blake's enormous frame blocked my view of the front yard. He was standing with his back toward me, hands on his hips, stetson tipped far back on his handsome head, gazing at the white-covered trees. He spun toward me, his deep brown eyes burrowing into mine.

"Hey, Alex. I was on my way to the department when you called. Looks like some vandals hit you hard last night, eh?"

I swallowed hard. "Yes. It's on every tree and shrub around the yard."

"Mm-hmm. Any idea who did it?"

"None. Never heard a thing."

"Mm-hmm. Wanna know what I think?"

"Lay it on me."

He shivered, then rubbed meaty hands up and down his arms. "Be happy to, but first, coffee? It was early, and I left without one. Besides, it's cold as a witch's tit..." He stopped, clamping his mouth shut.

My eyebrows shot up. "Hilarious, Blake. Fine. Come in, I'll make you a coffee."

"Hold the foamy genitalia, if you don't mind. Once was enough."

I couldn't hold back a chuckle. "Are you sure? I've almost mastered it."

It was his turn to laugh. We made our way past the antique furniture-stuffed living and dining rooms to the sunny kitchen. A short swath of toilet paper had cut loose and plastered itself against the kitchen nook window, followed by another.

"Who would do such a thing, Blake?" I asked as I prepped the Nespresso.

Blake raised his voice over the sounds of the coffee maker. "Teens, most likely. Pulling pre-Halloween stunts is my guess."

"Anyone else in town report vandalism?" I handed him a cup of steaming coffee.

He nodded his thanks, wrapping his hands around the mug. "Not that I know of. I'll check with the boys when I get to the station." He glanced around the kitchen. "Where's the tootie cat?"

"Sleeping upstairs."

"Ahh." He took a deep sip of the hot liquid, then asked, "How's Penny?"

My jaw clenched. "She's fine. Why do you ask?"

Blake shrugged a shoulder. "Just asking. I know she's a friend of yours...and you two have been through a lot recently. You know, demon hunting and all..."

He knew Penny was a witch. Although I hadn't fully admitted it, he knew Penny was involved recently when I was up to some necessary witchy business. I made excuses then, but poor Penny was beside herself with fear of being caught and thrown into the bowels of the castle and burning on the pyre.

Time to change the subject.

"So, what can you do about the vandalism on my property?"

Blake gulped back the rest of his coffee and slid the empty cup across the island. "I'll file an official report, but you should really put up security cameras, and maybe consider fencing your yard. Aside from the picket fences around your gardens out front, you're kind of exposed."

I stared at the diminishing coffee foam in my cup, frowning. I hated the idea of fencing the property. It would block the ocean view in the backyard, for one, and my friendly neighbors on either side of me. I loved sharing vegetables from my garden and chatting on the lounge chairs under the back arbor with them.

I wasn't a social butterfly, but I enjoyed the occasional barbecue with people from the neighborhood. I clung to the 'normal' side of my life outside the cauldron. Inside, the secrets were as deep as the cauldron itself.

"I'll call the security company today and have some cameras installed. I've been thinking about that anyway since..." I stopped short. My protection jars had been broken only a few weeks ago. I'd replaced the jars, which had also been dug up and now lay broken and empty. Blake was still on my list of suspects, so I didn't want to overshare.

"Since what?"

"Nevermind, not important." I finished my coffee and put the mugs in the sink.

Blake drew a breath and slid off the island stool. "Well, guess I'll get to the station and write this up. Do you need any help to clean up the trees?"

I thought about it for a millisecond, then shook my head. "No, it's okay. I can take care of that myself."

Blake's mouth tugged into a half smile. "Using magic, you mean?"

I gave him a little shove toward the door. "Mind your business, Sheraton." I returned his smile.

"Okay, okay. I can take the hint. Call me if you need help, though, ok?"

"Sure, Blake. You're on my speed dial, remember?"

He winked, making a victorious fist pump in the air.

CHAPTER
FOUR

BLAKE

Alex closed the door behind me as I hurried to my car. She'd been giving me the brush off since I tried to kiss her a few weeks ago, so I was really glad for the call. It was so good to see her again. In the flesh, this time, not just in the space of my mind reserved for private times that included a box of tissues and a good dose of hand cream.

I opened the door to my squad car and took another look at Alex's property. The trees were suffocating under the veil of tissue and I wondered who did it, and how long it took. Must have been hours. Strange that Alex had heard nothing because the toilet paper was strung right from the very top of the trees and down to the ground.

Someone had to be an excellent climber or...they used magic. Which could explain why she had heard no one rustling the trees.

I looked to the right, noticing the mound of dirt and

broken jar near the corner of the property, and wondered about that, too.

Who would have known the protection jars were there and broke them?

Not me. Not this time, anyway.

But I needed to ensure nothing could mess with my getting close to Alex.

As far as I could tell, she didn't suspect me of breaking the jars, and she definitely didn't suspect me of being a Witch Hunter, or she would have skipped town by now.

I've known Alex was a witch for weeks now, and had suspected Penny too, at first, then found out for sure later. I reported my findings to the High Commander of the Witch Hunters. An Order I was proud to belong to, as had my father. He and my mom had been killed by a witch. At least, that's what I was told, so it strengthened my belief that all witches are as evil as Earl Dagon professed, so many centuries ago when he laid down the law.

When it came to it, I couldn't turn Alexandra in. She and I had gotten fairly close when she was solving a case of demonic possession only a few weeks ago. Although I knew she had some amazing powers, I would rightfully possess as a Witch Hunter, I just couldn't imagine stripping them from her and burning that beautiful creature on the pyre.

I couldn't handle the thought of losing her.

I shifted my junk and slid into the car.

Penny, I didn't know, so it was her name on my lips when the High Commander—my boss, Sheriff Gordon Roberts—demanded one from me.

I was buying some time before capturing her, however. I had to make sure she had strong enough powers to warrant my stripping them from her. Also, I knew she was

Alex's best friend. If Alex ever found out it was me who turned Penny in, she'd hate me forever.

It was a damned-if-you-do type of situation that made me regret mentioning anything about finding a witch at all. My big, stupid head and grandiose ideas about being the first to accumulate a witch's powers after fifty-plus years of no witch sightings in Castle Point were kind of exciting.

Sheriff Roberts would not let it slide, however, so I either had to produce Penny or think of something—fast.

I leaned toward thinking fast.

Hopefully, it would be fast enough.

I turned on the ignition and headed for the station.

I PULLED into my parking stall at the station and walked inside. Sheriff Roberts spotted me walking through the bullpen and motioned for me to come into his office and close the door.

Dammit.

I was next in line for Sheriff Roberts' seat in the department, but I was far from his place in line as High Commander of the Witch Hunters. He was one of many hunters around the world that hadn't received a witch's powers, as witches everywhere got more and more clever about hiding in plain sight. The elder hunters had all but died off, the last of them either too old to use the powers they had, or too infirm to care.

Sheriff Roberts was an exceptionally tall man. His hair; white and close-cut, was the stark opposite of his dark skin and eyes. Besides his white hair, tiny eye lines and a creased forehead showed his age. He folded his hands and placed them on his desk. "Blake. The High Counsel of the Order of the Witch Hunters is getting impatient. You need to produce Penny, and you need to do it now."

My chest tightened. I wanted to run out the door, but who was I kidding? I opened my mouth in the first place, so of course they'd put the screws to me, eventually.

"I know, I know. I was just hoping for a little more time, you know, to find out more about her."

"You've had weeks, Sheraton. Our patience is thinner than the hair on Deputy Tom's head."

I glanced through the window at Tom, his balding noggin bent over some paperwork. I pursed my lips. "Yes, sir. It's just…"

"It's just nothing! You've had more than enough time. Produce the witch or risk being burned on the pyre yourself!" Spittle flew from the Sheriff's mouth and landed on his desk blotter.

I eyed the wet spots. "Yes sir. I will, sir."

"There's plenty of other Witch Hunters willing to do the job, Blake. If you think you're not up to the task…"

I shook my head. "No, sir. I found her. I'll produce her at the next meeting."

"Earlier than that, Sheraton! The full moon on All Hallows Eve is the time to perform the ritual!"

I clamped my mouth shut, drawing my lips into a thin line. "Yes, sir, that's still a few days away. There's time…"

The Sheriff leaned back in his chair, his eyes boring into me. Cold sweat dotted my temples and my guts churned. We sat in silence for several moments. I couldn't meet his eyes but could feel them assessing me.

I wished for the ability to read his thoughts and briefly wondered if that was one of Penny's powers.

He harrumphed, clearing his throat. "Dismissed." He grabbed a file from the corner of his desk and opened it.

I shot up, opened the door, and bolted for my office. Closing the door behind me, I sat, pondering my stupidity and my big mouth.

Rock, meet hard place.

"I'm sorry, Alex," I said under my breath as I pulled out the required form to file Alex's vandalism.

FIVE

ALEXANDRA

S hortly after Blake left, I called the security company to arrange for camera installation, then called Penny. I told her about the vandalism and asked her to meet me at the apothecary after her shift.

Then I called my next-door neighbor, Mrs. Willoughby, a retired schoolteacher, and told her about the vandalism. I asked if she could let the other neighbors know, in case anyone saw anything. She asked if I needed help to clean up the mess, but I told her I'd get to it later today.

No sense in putting actual effort into something that could easily be fixed with magic.

I got ready, woke up Blackjack, and headed to my therapy practice. My office was next to the apothecary. I had a few clients on the agenda, mainly my usual, nobody with any entity attachments, thank the Goddess. Although releasing entities from unsuspecting non-mages was rather fun, I'd had my fill of demons lately.

Blackjack was in his usual sleeping position in the office

lounge when I finished up for the day. I asked my reception-ist, Maggy, to lock up, scooped up Blackjack, and headed next door.

Penny and Teddy were already there, Teddy seeing to the last of the shop patrons of the day. Penny refrained from popping bottle tops and sniffing, but I could tell it wasn't easy. She stood beside the front counter, hands clasped in front of her curvy belly. She smiled when I walked in.

"Alex! Blackjack! Ooh, come here, you sweet little kitty witty." Penny pulled the sleepy cat from my arms and went to town on his head, rigorously trying to stroke a purr from him. He wasn't having it. He struggled free of her grasp and scooted behind the front counter.

Penny snickered. "Ahh, cranky as ever."

"Control the red-haired beast, woman. For the love of all things familiar." Blackjack's voice pushed through my mind. I laughed.

"What did he say?" Penny asked under her breath, smiling at the last patron as she left the shop.

"That I need to control you. He called you a beast."

Penny guffawed and chased Blackjack around the shop, calling, "Here, kitty, kitty. Nice kitty. Aunty Penny wants to smother you with love, so let me, dammit!"

Teddy could barely lock the front door and turn down the lights, she was laughing so hard. Blackjack scooted up my legs, past my arms, and tucked behind my neck, hiding under my hair.

"Hey! You mangey brat! Ow!" I peeled his claws from my skin and shimmied him into my arms.

"That woman needs a leash," Blackjack panted. *"And I'm not mangey! Honestly, you're just as bad as she is."*

"Good Goddess, you two. Let's go!" I held Blackjack as

we stepped into the back room of the shop. Draco and Lucius rose to greet us, then bowed. *"Mistresses."*

Blackjack leaped from my arms and scurried under the desk, avoiding the massive hellhounds. The Bull Mastiff glamor they normally wore was off. Their massive heads, razor-sharp teeth, and gut—ripping claws were out on full display. Their natural look was rather terrifying. It didn't stop any of us, however. We each gave them some pats and stroked their scaly skin. Since I had vanquished their wannabe demon owner a few years ago—who was Teddy's ex-boyfriend—the hell hounds were now Teddy's prized possession and protectors of our secrets.

"Hello, boys," I cooed, stroking their heads. I turned to the girls. "Okay witches, we have a little clea-up to do at my place."

Penny clapped her hands together, her generous breasts jiggling. Teddy hopped up and down, her black platform boots smacking against the wood floor and purple pigtails shaking.

Teddy piped up. "Penny told me about the t.p. party. Super duper not cool, dude. Like, who would do such a terrible thing to innocent trees?"

"Wish I knew, Teddy. I'm having cameras installed, so if they ever come back, I'll see."

"Does Teddy know the spell?" Penny asked. Teddy—not a natural-born witch—was pretty fresh out of Glamor 101, but she had been learning to focus her intention on other things, too.

"Teddy's been using her intention practice for cleaning up the shop. This isn't any different, really. And it will be excellent practice for her."

Penny eyed me, hands on her hips. "Outdoors. For all of

Castle Point to see. Don't think that *may* be an issue? What if Mr. Hotty Sheriff is watching?"

"I get it, Pen. But it's already dark, so, I figured, with a good watch cat and a cloaking spell, we can have the trees freed in no time."

Penny huffed out a breath. "Okay, Alex. Do you know where we can get a good watch cat?" She teased, peering under the desk.

"Hilarious, woman's red-haired devil friend."

I clap my hands together. "Blackjack volunteers!"

"Oh dear Goddess, why am I tasked with watching over this one? How much more of this punishment must I endure?"

I laughed, slapping a hand on my knee. Penny and Teddy eyed me, then Blackjack, quizzically.

"Nevermind Mr. Cranky Cat. Let's head over to my place. I have all the ingredients ready for making fresh protection jars, and at least a case of wine. Pen, do you think Cathy would want to join us?" I asked, referring to Penny's wife.

"For the magic part? Not a chance. That falls under the need-to-know rule we have. For wine? Heck yes, she would. I'll text her."

"Great! Let's go, Blackjack!"

On hearing his name, Blackjack eyed the hell hounds curled up on their massive dog beds, snoozing. He scooted to the door, then through when I opened it.

When the four of us entered the front, our eyes barely had to adjust. Darkness cloaked the normally bright shop.

A *thwack* sound made us jump, even Blackjack.

"What the heckin' heck was that?"

"I don't know, Teddy. I..."

Thwack

We jumped again. This time, the sound came from the front windows. They vibrated.

Thwack

Shudder.

Thwack

Shudder.

Penny screeched, "Geez, Alex! Someone's throwing eggs at the shop!"

I peered at the front windows. Long streaks of bright yellow yolks and gooey whites ran down. Before I could open my mouth, Penny had unlocked the front door and raced outside, hollering.

"Get the hell away from here, or I'm gonna..." she huffed, sentence unfinished.

Teddy and I ran to the sidewalk and watched as Penny ran after at least two darkly cloaked people, maybe more.

"Penny! Come back!" I yelled. She stopped short, red hair flailing around her before turning on her heel and heading back to the shop.

"I coulda had them, Alex!" she wheezed.

"Could ya though?" I laughed, despite my shock at being vandalized—again.

"Who was it? Did you see?" Teddy asked, craning her neck and peering into the dark street.

Penny took a deep breath. "Nope. Someone wearing all black, though. Actually, I think it was a group of someones. One of them turned back as I was closing in on them." I tried to suppress a giggle, knowing Penny had gotten nowhere near the group. "But all I saw were two weird, glowing eyes. Must have been wearing Halloween costumes."

I surveyed the gooey egg mess coating the windows.

Great, just great.

"Maybe you need to call the hot Sheriff?" Penny asked, wiggling her eyebrows.

I shook my head. "Nah. I'll just take a couple of pictures and send them over to him. Not much he could do. Likely it's just kids high on pre-Halloween chocolate being idiots." I took out my phone, turned on the flash, and snapped a few pics, texting them to Blake. I waited a moment or two for a reply but didn't get one. I refrained from pouting and put the phone on 'do not disturb'.

Penny stood, hands on hips, peering at me.

"What?" I asked

"Why your shop, Alex? And your house? I don't see any scrambled eggs on the other buildings."

She had a point.

The four of us looked side to side at the offices and buildings next to the two of mine. My therapy practice was attached by a wall to the apothecary. The windows of my practice were much smaller, and the shades were usually drawn to protect my client's privacy. I walked to the windows. Sure enough, there was a gooey mess of eggs there, too. I snapped a couple of pictures and sent those to Blake as well.

"What do you want us to do, Alex? Should I get the bucket and wash up?" Teddy asked.

I had an idea.

"No, Teddy. Actually, I think this is a wonderful opportunity for you to flex your magic muscle. Can you intend for the windows to be cleaned?"

"Alex!" Penny scolded. "Have you lost your ever-witchy mind? It's one thing to use magic in your quiet neighborhood, but here, in town?" Penny shook her head.

I glanced up and down the street. It wasn't very late in the evening, but it was dark and the streets deserted. Once five o'clock hit Castle Point, the town rolled up the red carpet and tucked it away for the night.

"I think we're good, Pen. You and Blackjack can play watch-cat together while I help Teddy."

Blackjack narrowed his eyes at me when Penny scooped him up. "Okay, fine. It's your life on the pyre. Ready, kitty?" She stroked his head and neck in her usual jovial firmness, exactly what Blackjack hated, and she knew it. He refrained from commenting and swiped at her nose. She flipped her head back and giggled.

"Missed me, missed me, now you gotta kiss me..." she singsonged before planting a big, squishy kiss on his head. Blackjack's ears went flat, but he settled into her arms, resigned.

"Okay, Teddy. I want you to focus intently on the eggs. *Intend*—not for the eggs to disappear, but for the windows to be shiny and clean. Think you can do that?"

Teddy nodded, her purple pigtails whipping her face. She took a deep breath and stared at the windows, fists clenched at her sides. She breathed in and out deeply, focusing on her intention.

"Good Teddy, you're doing great. Whenever you're ready, say the spell." I instructed quietly.

She whispered:

"Goddess good, Goddess great, intend with me, cooperate.
Clear the mess in front of me, make things fresh and clean again."

Teddy gasped as the mess of egg yolks and jelly whites disappeared. Clean, sparkling windows reflected the nearby streetlight.

"Great job, Teddy! You did it!" I grabbed her arm and

pulled her in for a hug. Penny gave a quiet 'whoop.' "Okay, let's get over to my place and fix the mess over there, shall we?"

~

PENNY DROVE her own car to my place with Blackjack in the front seat. I asked Teddy to grab the hell hounds—glamoring them first, of course—and ride with me. The hounds would be better watchdogs than Blackjack and added security for my house until the cameras could be installed. Blackjack was not super keen on the idea of having the 'big drooling beasts' in our home, but I promised him extra tuna for putting up with the hounds. He grudgingly agreed.

Ocean View Drive was in relative darkness, aside from a few street lamps. As we drove closer to my house, I pointed to the lamps and flicked my finger, turning the lights off. Now, my house, and about fifty feet on either side of it, was in total darkness.

Teddy clapped. "Coolio! Can you teach me to do that, too?"

I smiled, parking in front of the house. "It's as easy as intending for clean windows, honestly."

"But you did it so fast! I have to really think about it first." She frowned.

"The more you practice, the faster you get. Practice makes perfect." I smiled again, resisting the urge to stroke her crazy hair. I knew I'd never have a daughter of my own, and although Teddy was old enough to be my sister, not my daughter, my natural mothering instincts seemed to kick in where she was concerned.

We walked up the front path. The white house, the white picket fences surrounding the gardens, and the white streams of toilet paper glowed in the thin crescent moonlight. Hardly a whisper of t.p. had been freed from the tree's grasp during the day.

"Golly," Teddy breathed.

Penny chimed in, holding Blackjack out of the hellhound's reach. "Good Goddess, that's a Costco load of asswipe. What a waste. Maybe we could roll it all up again and sell it to the Doomsday Preppers."

I slapped a hand to my mouth, suppressing a giggle, and led them around the back.

"Let's start back here. Draco and Lucius prowl the perimeter, please. Bark once if you see someone approaching, but don't attack!" The hounds bowed their heads and scurried off. "Blackjack, head up to the roof. You can see further that way. Howl if you see anyone, and for Goddess's sake, don't fall asleep on your watch!"

Blackjack twisted his whiskers smugly. *"Fine. As long as I'm out of drool-shot, I will cooperate 'Mistress'."* He attempted a feeble bow before jumping into a nearby tree, scurrying up a large branch and onto the roof. We watched as he climbed the steep roof to the highest point, and sat, surveying the yard and street below.

Satisfied, I turned to Teddy. "Teddy, you start with the shrubs, then join me and Penny to work on the bigger trees."

Teddy nodded. "What am I intending for, exactly?"

I thought about it for a couple of seconds, tugging gently on my earring as I did so. "Intend for the paper to fall off the shrubs, then gather it up and put it in the recycling bin by the side of the house. Think you can manage that?"

Teddy nodded again and set off toward the furthest shrub. Penny and I watched as Teddy focused on the shrub, just as she had on the windows. When the paper easily dropped off the shrub in a billowy cloud, we knew she had it. She gave a tiny squeak, beaming at us. We gave her a silent double thumbs up and did the same to the trees.

In no time at all, we had freed the trees of their burden and gathered the t.p. into piles for recycling. Even after Penny lifted Teddy into the bin to stomp the contents down with her clunky boots, it wouldn't all fit, so we had to bag up the rest for next week's recycling collection.

"Should we replace your protection jars now?" Teddy asked.

I hesitated, having replaced them recently after Blackjack found them dug up and broken, and the contents spilled out. "I'm not sure it would do any good, to be honest."

Penny pointed a finger skyward. "I know your recipe. What if we added Dragon's Blood? I can't think of a demon or beast that could get past that!"

She had a point. "What about Draco and Lucius? Could I even have the hounds on the property with Dragon's Blood protecting it?"

Penny moved her finger to her chin and tapped. "Hmmm. Good point. Teddy? Any idea? They're your hounds and you are the Master Herbalist."

Teddy parroted Penny and tapped her finger on her chin. "Thinking... thinking,...I think it would work! We could let them sniff the bottle first, to be sure. If they are going to react to it, they'd likely do so the minute the bottle was open."

"Okay, great. Let's go inside and prepare them. Teddy, get the hounds and Blackjack. Penny, get the wine." We went inside and got to work. The hounds didn't react to the dried ingredient. Instead, they seemed eager to lap it up.

Teddy grabbed the steaks from the fridge and fed them instead.

Within each jar, we placed:

1/2 tsp dried Dragon's Blood

3 sprigs of Rosemary,

3 sprigs of Basil,

2 sprigs of Fennel

2 sprigs of Dill

1 Bay Leaf

1 Fern leaf

1 pinch of salt

And sealed each jar with black candle wax. We dug the holes even deeper into the rich, black earth, placing the jars in the deep holes, and saying the protection prayer over each one:

"Goddess of the North, South, East, and West, come forth.
Place your blessings on these jars, so they may protect this
property,
from the forces of evil and shelter all who dwell within.
So mote it be."

We went back inside to relax in the living room and wait for Cathy to arrive. Teddy gave a low whistle as she surveyed the antique furnishings strewn through the house.

"Wow, it's like a museum of old-timey stuff in here." She sat on the chaise in front of the bay window.

I reached for the drapes and closed them before turning on the lamps. The hounds had curled up in front of the fire. I flicked my finger at the fireplace, lighting it.

"Most of it came with the house, which turned my mom into a collector. She added several pieces before..." I cut off.

"Before what?" Teddy asked.

I glanced at Penny, now settled on the couch, texting Cathy to come over. She looked up and tilted her head toward Teddy. "Tell her, Alex."

I nodded. "Before my mom was admitted to Lexington Psychiatric Hospital."

Teddy's eyes bulged. "What? Oh good golly, Alex, that's so sad! What happened?"

I looked at Penny again. Her eyes softened as she offered a small smile. "It's kind of a long story," she said. "And not super easy for Alex to talk about."

"Oh, I'm sorry, Alex. I don't mean to pry."

"No, it's ok, Teddy, but Penny's right. It's a long story and not a very pleasant one."

Teddy cocked her head and smiled. "I'm always around if you want to chi-chat, Alex. You've been such a tremendous help to me, for gosh's sake. Expelling my stupid-head, wanna-be demon boyfriend and hiring me to be your herbalist...I just appreciate the heck out of you!" Teddy jumped off the chaise to give me a squeeze.

Penny cleared her throat. Imitating the Queen of England, she said; "It occurs to me we have another witch in our midst, Alexaannndraa. One that has proven her qualifications thusly."

I peered at Penny over Teddy's purple hair. "What you talkin' 'bout, Pen?"

Penny stood and made a grandiose gesture, sweeping her arms wide and bowing. "I give you Castle Point Coven member number three; Theodora Cunningham!"

Teddy turned to Penny, squealing like a piglet and hopping like a bunny. "Oh my Goddess, oh my Goddess, oh my Goddess! Really? EEEEEEEEEE!"

Penny nodded. "Absosmurfly, wee one. Do I hear a

second to the nomination, High Priestess?" Penny addressed me. We had only recently formed a Coven of two —well, three if you counted Blackjack which, technically speaking, wouldn't really count—and Penny named me High Priestess.

Forming a Coven in a world where witchcraft was illegal might be fatal, but my thoughts on the subject shifted when I brought Penny with me to Lex Psych and we worked together to help my mom out from under a demon's curse. The two of us had gotten further than I had in twenty years of trying alone.

"Strength in numbers." Cressy's previous advice floated through my mind. Weighing the risk of building a coven with the reward of helping my mother tipped the scales in my mother's favor.

Selfishly, I approved. "Here, here! Welcome, Theodora!" I gave her another squeeze. Penny wrapped her arms around both of us and did the same, forcing the air from our lungs.

We broke apart hearing a knock on the door and Penny's wife, Cathy, stepped in.

"Hey, Cathy! You're just in time!" I gave her a warm hug. Teddy did likewise before Penny butted in to give her wife a smooch and a squeeze. Cathy's smaller frame fit perfectly within Penny's larger one. Her short-cropped dark hair and piercing blue eyes also complemented Penny's long, curly red locks and amber-green eyes.

Cathy had known about Penny's witchy side right from the start. Although Cathy had also grown up with the false belief that all witches were evil—as most of the non-mage population had—she fell deeply in love with Penny. They sealed the deal and Cathy's silence when they married five years ago.

They were the perfect couple, and I often wished I could find 'the one' they had. Someone who I could trust with my secrets. My thoughts flitted to Blake. He knew the truth about me, at least part of it, and so far, he hadn't turned me in. He was strong, incredibly handsome, and did something to my insides that I could only equate to eating caramel—filled chocolates and drinking a good bottle of wine.

But, in Blake's case, the risks outweighed the rewards. I knew, now that the previous business of demon—busting with Blake was over, that I'd have to say goodbye and cast a forgetting spell over the tall, dark, handsome man.

I should have done it weeks ago.

The thought of doing so soured the taste of the wine I was currently sipping with the gals and left a hollow pit in my stomach. I had put it off long enough. I made a mental note to perform the spell sooner than later.

That note would have to stick.

I watched Cathy and Penny as they lay on the floor, sipping their wine, their upper bodies supported by the hellhounds. Teddy was curled up on the chaise, Blackjack in her lap, purring loudly. My heart filled with the warmth only good friends and family could bring.

And a coven.

Law and the Witch Hunters be damned.

I wanted more of this, and I intended to have it.

CHAPTER

SIX

ALEXANDRA

The ladies stayed well after the bottle of wine had been shared, talking, laughing, and cuddling the animals and each other. I invited them to sleep over, but Cathy, Penny, and Teddy had all switched to water hours before leaving since they had to work in the morning and Teddy had a shop to open. Cathy drove her car home alone. Penny dropped Teddy at her apartment before heading home, leaving me at home with Draco, Lucius, and Blackjack. The hounds—my new security team—stayed on alert downstairs. Blackjack normally slept on the couch, but as he refused to be alone near the droolers, he curled up with me.

Earl Dagon haunted my dreams.

His face blended and changed to Blake's, then back again. Either man reached out to grab me, insisting I be with him. When the image was Blake, my heart filled with excitement and promise. When the image shifted to

Dagon's, it plummeted into despair. My dreams were a battleground of evil and not—so—bad.

Pulse racing and sweat bleeding off my body, I tossed and turned, finally waking when the early morning light shone through a crack in the curtains. Blackjack, likely tired of competing for bed space, had left the bedroom during the night. Sensing I was awake, he padded into the bedroom and hopped up to take up his usual morning position on my chest.

His weight was both comforting and annoying. I pulled my hands out from under the swe-stained sheets and stroked his fur. I'd have to wash the sheets again.

"Bad dreams again, woman?"

"If this keeps up, I'll have to hire a laundry service."

"Hire a housekeeper while you're at it. You still haven't addressed the dust bunny situation, and they're multiplying."

"I'll take it under advisement. Now shove off, oh caring Familiar. I have to get to the office."

"Yes, Mistress."

I rolled my eyes at him. "You could take a page or two from Draco and Lucius, you snobby cranky pants. How are those two, anyway?"

"Ask them yourself, woman. I'm your familiar, not your secretary." Blackjack stalked out of the room, tail high in the air.

I tossed my sweat-soaked t-shirt at him. "Helpful as usual!" Hopping into the shower, I let the hot, steamy water wash away the bad dream. Blake's face entered my vision, causing goose-nips to rise, despite the hot water rushing over them. The mental note I made the night before clicked in my mind.

The forgetting spell.

I'd have to perform the damn thing tonight. Maybe then

41

I can wash that man and his lavender, mint scent right down the drain.

Except I used the same shampoo.

Clearly, I'd have to remove it from the inventory and create something new.

Something less...Blake.

I finished getting ready and headed downstairs. The hounds sat at the bottom of the stairs, bowing when they saw me.

"Mistress."

"Hey, boys. Quiet night?"

"Yes, Mistress. No activity to report."

"Good news, thank you. I'll let you out the back door. I have a couple of steaks in the fridge for you when you come back inside."

They bowed again and followed me into the kitchen. Blackjack also followed. Refusing to set a paw on the ground anywhere close to the hounds, he jumped and leaped from table to chair to furniture piece like a child playing a game of 'lava floor.' Such a dork.

After copious coffees, feeding the hounds, and tidying up from the evening before. I rolled the recycling bin to the curb and drove to the office with Blackjack on the seat. It was still fairly early. I knew my receptionist, Maggie, wouldn't be at the office yet, nor Teddy at the shop.

When I approached my two businesses, my stomach dropped to the floor.

Someone had spray-painted "WITCH" in bright red across both buildings.

I screeched to a stop, Blackjack slipping off the seat onto the floor.

"Hey!"

"Sorry," I said absently, staring out the window. I saw

movement in my periphery. Local shop owners further down the street were parking and opening shop. I spun to look behind me. Other owners doing the same up the street. "Goddess, help me." I rasped, pulling my car into a stall.

Who did this, and how many people have already seen it?

"Did what? Seen what? Ooh...!" Blackjack climbed up on the car dash and spotted the incriminating paint job. I clamored from the car, Blackjack following, tucking his tail before getting it pinched in the door. Other sho-keeps were arriving, including Teddy. Her eyes were as wide as the harvest moon when she saw the building.

I had to get rid of the paint, and fast.

Without the entire street knowing.

I wondered again who had already seen it, and what they would think.

Teddy joined me and we sashayed across the street, so as not to draw any unwanted attention. When we stepped in front of the building, she clasped my hand. I was grateful for the warmth and comfort, but couldn't draw my eyes from the messy scrawl. The paint was dry, which meant it had to have been there for hours.

Which also meant the chances of someone seeing it were greater.

My heart thudded hard against my chest. I brought my free hand up to it, clenching my coat. There were other markings alongside the red 'witch'.

Symbols.

The same type of symbols Mitch Myles had drawn on his cell walls and my mother on the notepad only a few weeks ago. I stepped a little closer and studied them. They weren't the same, but they were close.

And they had to go.

I looked at Teddy, eyes still huge, and nodded. "You know what to do," I said. She nodded back and closed her eyes. "Wait!" I grabbed my phone from my coat pocket and snapped a few pictures. I would send them to Blake later.

I briefly wondered if Blake was the culprit. A mixture of fear and dismay roiled through my belly, and the piercing tang of puke rose in my throat. I swallowed it down and grabbed Teddy's hand again, glancing up and down the street.

Now or never.

We closed our eyes and said the same spell Teddy had the evening before to wipe the windows clean. When we opened our eyes, the evidence of my true existence was gone.

"Alex..." Teddy started, but I stopped her.

"Just act like nothing happened, Teddy. Go to work as usual. If anyone mentions anything, just act as if you don't have a clue what they're talking about."

Teddy nodded and slipped her key into the door, unlocking the shop. I went next door and did the same at my office. I kept the reception room light off and walked to my desk. Sitting down, I finally let out the breath I had been holding.

I decided I would send the picture to Blake. He hadn't yet responded to the egg pictures I'd sent the night before. At least, I didn't think so. Then I remembered I had put my phone on do—not—disturb after sending him the pictures and didn't take it off again. He likely replied, and I just hadn't seen it.

I grabbed my phone and slid the screen down, turning off the DND.

A flurry of messages and missed phone calls appeared.

I missed a call and a couple of texts from Blake, but the majority were from Cathy.

Twent-four calls, to be exact.

Spikes of fear jolted me into action. I didn't bother to listen to the messages she had left, I just hit her number. She answered on the first ring.

"Alex! Oh, thank God, I've been calling you for hours."

"Cathy! I'm so sorry. My phone was muted. What's going on?"

"It's Penny! She...didn't come home last night!" Cathy choked on her words.

"What?"

"After I left for home, I crashed and...didn't even notice that she hadn't come home...until early this morning. I thought maybe she slept over at... Teddy's, but I don't have her number. I've been calling Penny for hours, and...no answer!" Her words flew out in a rush between ragged breaths and sobs.

"Did you try 'Find My Phone'?"

"Yes, and nothing! Not a trace."

"Okay Cathy, just breathe for a minute. I'm at the office. I'll check in with Teddy and get right back to you, ok?"

"Mm.. okay." Cathy hung up. I thought of running next door, but a call would be quicker. I jabbed at Teddy's number. She answered, mid-ring.

"Alex? What's wrong?" Her psychic skills were blossoming.

"Penny. Did she sleep at your place last night?"

"No, she dropped me off and left. Why, what's happening?"

"She's missing."

"Oh, dear Goddess, do you think..."

"I can't go there, Teddy. Not right now. I'm going to talk

45

to Blake. You can close the shop and hang a sign, I don't care. We have to find her." I hung up and called Cathy back with the not-so-great news. She couldn't answer me through her sobs.

"Cathy, I'm going to talk to Blake, okay? Then I'll come over. You just sit tight until I get there, ok?"

"Okay, Alex...please...hurry."

I promised her I would and hung up. Checking my messages from Blake, the only one is about the pictures. "More vandalism?" It said. Then "I'll file this with your other report." *Fat lot of good that would do*, I muttered.

I had to think.

My protection jars broken, the eggs, the t.p., and now the blasphemous message painted on my buildings, and now Penny—a witch—is missing.

Who did it point to?

Blake?

He knew Penny was a witch. Had he arrested her? That had to be it.

The Dagon-loving bastard.

I felt my ancestral Dagon's blood boil in my veins. My hands became instantly red hot as if I'd just pulled from a flame. I stared down at them. I'd already used the evil power buried deep within me to destroy my high school and put half the football team in the hospital, including Blake. After that, with Cressy's forgetting spell, and a stint in Juvie, I'd learned to control that side of me.

I would take everything Cressy ever taught me to control the rage I felt rolling through me now. If Blake were in front of me, I couldn't promise I'd keep it leashed.

But I had to, for Penny.

I needed to find out what happened to her. Blake—if he

wasn't responsible—may be the only person who could help me.

Again.

A realization flooded over me. The forgetting spell. If Blake handled Penny's disappearance, then there was no way I could cast the spell now. Whether or not he was responsible, I would need his help.

The bile I had previously swallowed rapidly rose in the back of my throat. I bolted out of my office into the washroom and retched into the toilet. Falling to my knees, I let the tears that had been stinging my eyes flow and retched again.

Penny's adorable face swam before me. She was the psychic one of our small clan, and I could sure use her abilities now. I straightened up, rinsed out my mouth and face, and walked into the reception area. Maggie had arrived.

"You okay, boss?" Concern tinted her voice.

"No, Maggie. Could you please cancel all my appointments today, and possibly for the next week? I've got…a bug." I didn't need to concern my non-mage receptionist with my other-world issues.

One non-mage Deputy Sheriff was enough.

I pulled on my coat, grabbed Blackjack, and headed for the Sheriff's department for a little heart-to-heart with the man who could be my worst enemy or my best ally.

SEVEN

BLAKE

I was hiding in my office from Sheriff Roberts, looking over the pictures Alexandra had sent me the night before. The egg salad streaking her windows I could brush off as a bunch of kids, up to the usual Halloween antics. The red letters spelling "Witch" were another thing.

I compared Alex's picture with one texted to me earlier, by a local passing by the shop, who felt it was their "civic duty" to report their finding. Not because of the vandalism to someone's establishment, no. Because witch sightings and reportings are an expected practice, worldwide.

A rock-hard lump formed in my throat. Another one settled firmly at the bottom of my gut.

I called the number of the person who had sent me the text. It was old Thomas McCafferty. He had been out walking his Dachshund when he spotted the red paint and got closer for a better look and texted me the picture. Thankfully, he had my number from a previous incident he had reported—Mrs. Twillinger taking a baseball bat to his prized '57 Chevy Bel Air and hadn't sent the picture to anyone else. I gave Thomas explicit instructions not to breathe a word of it to anyone.

"I get yer drift, Sheriff Blake. You'll be wanting to sneak up on the nasty gal without her knowing—or turn her over to the Witch Hunters, I'd expect." Thomas stated, knowingly.

My stomach lurched. I struggled to find words, let alone an authoritative voice. "Yes...that's right, Thomas. Listen, I want you to just forget you ever saw the...paint. Can you do that? Just leave everything up to me. Not a word to anyone, understand?"

Thomas said he did.

I'd have to trust him on that point.

I'd just hung up the phone when Alexandra barged into the station. Loud voices came from the front desk lieutenant. I looked through my office window, watching her bolt past him, through the bullpen toward my office, 'Large Larry' puffing behind her. I stood when she reached the door, and let herself in.

"Sorry, boss. She just pushed past me." Larry huffed.

"No worries, Larry. I'll handle it." I closed the door. The lump in my gut was joined by another.

"Hey, Alex. I got your texts."

She rushed at me, hands on her hips, peering up at me. There was a fire in her eyes I hadn't seen before. Her hair spilled around her shoulders, her rapid movements wafting the scent of roses around the room, landing at my groin.

"What the hell, Blake? What did you do with Penny?"

"I didn't...wait, what?"

"Penny's *missing*, Blake. She didn't make it home last night after...she was at my place. You took her, didn't you? Where is she?" She poked my chest with one finger. I backed up, cornered like a caged cat. Tears that had threatened to fall from Alex's eyes finally let go. She wiped at her face furiously.

"Alex, I don't have a clue where Penny is. Did you call her wife? Her work?"

"Cathy called me, Blake. That's how I know. I've checked all the usual places. She's not anywhere. *What did you do with her?*" She practically shouted. I put a finger to my lips and led her to a chair.

"Alex, I swear to you, I don't know where Penny is. What makes you think I would know, anyway?"

"Because you know she's a witch! I know you do! And you're the law, Blake. In case you forgot." Alex's cheeks glistened with tear tracks.

I flopped into my chair and blew out a breath. The stones in my throat and gut moved into my head and smashed around. *What the hell was going on?* I mean, I knew I hadn't taken Penny. I was trying to think of creative ways to get out of that mess.

But if I hadn't taken her—who had?

My eyes flicked to the wall between me and Sheriff Roberts's office. I'd have to have a talk with him, right-stat-pronto. But first, I'd have to convince Alex it wasn't me who took Penny and give her some assurances.

"Alex," I soothed, my voice low, "I swear to God, I do not know where Penny is, and I didn't take her."

Alex leaned back in the chair, eyes blinking rapidly. "Then who did, Blake? Who else knows about her—about us?"

I shook my head, pursing my lips, wishing I could zipper them shut, but I had to be honest. I also had to be prepared. Honesty was the best policy, but in this case, it meant losing any chance I had to be with Alexandra, ever. I closed my eyes.

"The Witch Hunters know."

I heard Alex suck in a breath. I opened my eyes and prepared for the backlash. Alex just stared at me, realization flooding her face.

"You're...you're one of *them*?" Her voice was hushed. I slowly nodded my head.

"Yeah...'fraid so..." Until this moment, I had always been proud to be part of the worldwide Order. My father had been the High Commander of our chapter until his death, and I hoped to fill his shoes, one day.

Now, looking at Alexandra's face, I was no longer sure.

According to Earl Dagon's lore, witches were supposed to be evil, vile creatures. How could someone like Alexandra —a witch—be so wonderful and so evil at the same time? It didn't quite fit what I was taught.

But what about the witch who killed my parents? I mean, you'd have to be pretty vile to leave an eighteen-year-old orphan behind...

The rocks between my temples thudded harder.

"This entire time, you've been a Witch Hunter, Blake?" Alex's tone was quiet, but firm.

"Since my parents were killed by a witch, yes." I felt like making a point, reminding Alex of the only fact I knew—or was told—about my parents.

"A witch didn't kill your parents, Blake. I stand by my refusal to believe that load of crap." Alex's eyes bore into mine. I wanted to come to my parent's defense but was torn between defending a truth I was *told*, to trying to salvage what I could of my current relationship with Alex.

I chose Alex.

For now.

"Alex, look. I'm sorry I didn't tell you sooner, but I had my reasons."

"Yeah, so you could get closer to me and hopefully expose my witch friends."

That stung. But it wasn't far from the truth. "No, I didn't tell you because I didn't want to ruin our...friendship. I have a lot of respect for you, Alex, despite what you are."

Alex threw up her hands, her eyes bulging. "*Despite?* For the love of the Goddess, Blake. *I saved you from a demon attack.* If I wasn't what I am, you'd be dead!" She stood up and took a step toward the door.

I had to act fast.

"Alex, wait. I'm sorry, okay? I'm indebted to you. Honestly, I'm very grateful." She paused, hand on the doorknob. "Please, let me help you find Penny, okay? I feel responsible."

Alex turned and looked at me.

"Your kind of help. I don't need."

She swept open the door and stalked out.

CHAPTER

EIGHT

BLAKE

The meeting with Alexandra had me riled. I know I had messed up, and admitting that was pure torture. Certain that she'd never want to see me again, knowing I was a Witch Hunter. But the part about Penny missing—that was worse.

Sheriff Roberts returned from whatever meetings he had going on. As soon as I knew he was in his office, I stalked out, walked into his, closed the door, then the blinds on the window between his office and the bullpen. He watched me, his eyebrow quirked.

"Sheraton? What can I help you with?"

I drew a huge breath, clasping my fists at my side. "Penny is missing, sir. And, I didn't take her."

He narrowed his eyes at me. "You're certain she's missing? How do you know for sure?"

"Her wife alerted a mutual friend to her disappearance. I just received the news." The muscles in my jaw constricted.

"I see. So, she must have gotten wind of your intention to take her then. Who have you talked to?"

"No one, sir. The only people who know her name are from the Order."

He flicked his eyes from me to his desk. "Are you insinuating that another hunter took her?"

"I have to assume so, sir. Since it wasn't me."

"I see. Interesting."

"Isn't it, though? Excuse me sir, but are you telling me you do not know who may have taken Penny? Or where she is now?"

He looked smug. "None, Sheraton. Not yet, anyway. I have to assume that, if a hunter did take her, I'll be getting word of that shortly. But don't forget the possibility that the woman is simply missing."

I opened and closed my fists. My fingers had gone numb. Penny's disappearing for no apparent reason seemed as logical as peanut butter and pickles. "Can you let me know if another hunter has taken her, sir, when you find out?"

He leaned back in his chair, crossing his arms. "Blake, if another hunter took her, it's because he has grown impatient, waiting for you to do what you were assigned to do. It's your loss. Her powers will belong to another. That's all there is to it." He stared me down.

Clearly, if I was going to find Penny, I was on my own.

"If she's in the castle dungeon, how long before the ritual?" *I may still have some time*.

"The ritual will be performed on the full moon of Hallow's Eve. If she is in the dungeon, you will not be granted access, Sheraton. You can attend the ritual, but your loss is your loss." He picked up the phone, showing an end to our conversation.

I nodded and left his office, grabbed my stetson and coat, and walked out the door.

I needed to see Alex.

I needed to find Penny.

ALEXANDRA

I stormed out of Blake's office, out the door of the Sheriff's department, and into my car. There, I grabbed the steering wheel and bawled.

Blake was a Witch Hunter.

Blake had lied. Or at least, kept the truth from me.

All this time, I'd been living under the assumption that he was just a cop, who had the power to turn me over to the hunters, ending my life.

This was far worse. He *was* a hunter. Of course, he'd have to expose me at some point.

But he didn't, did he?

He exposed Penny instead. And now she was missing. My heart thudded hard inside my chest. The flow of blood through my body ramped up, heat stabbing the back of my eyes.

What if Penny was already dead?

No. I wiped my eyes and started the car. I refused to believe it. Prickly heat fired in the cauldron of my belly. I had to find her. I had to try. Punching Teddy's number into my phone, I started for home. Teddy picked up, her voice floating through my car's stereo.

"Hi, Alex! Any luck?"

"Teddy. Can you get over to my house?"

"Sure, of course. Anything I can bring?"

"Just yourself—for now. Quickly, okay?" I hit the 'end' button on the car's display.

As I drove, the events of the past couple of days splintered my mind. The toilet paper, the eggs, the red spray paint, Penny missing, and now Blake's confession.

The Witch Hunters. *They just had to know about me, too.* And they were teasing me with their juvenile antics.

But why? Why would they bother to taunt me, if they already knew? They'd just take me, wouldn't they? Like they took Penny?

Assuming it was them.

Blake said he had nothing to do with her disappearance, but that didn't mean he didn't know who did and where she was. He said he didn't, but I trusted nothing coming out of his damn sexy mouth now, so I certainly wasn't going to trust that. I mean, he said he wasn't going to turn me in, he had promised, but judging from the vandalism, I'd have to assume he broke that promise.

My desire to turn him into a warty toad burned as hot as a candle flame. At the very least, a forgetting spell. I briefly wished I'd done it sooner, like weeks ago. I slapped my hand against the steering wheel. If I had done it sooner, Blake wouldn't have reported Penny to the Witch Hunters and she wouldn't be missing now.

It was my fault.

Tears threatened to burst, and my stomach retched. I wanted to cry and hurl but I wouldn't give myself the satisfaction. I was more determined than ever to find Penny and get her back—alive.

Cathy was sitting on my front porch swing when I arrived. She was shivering, her lips practically blue.

"Cathy! You're turning blue. Let's get you inside."

"Alex..." Her teeth chattered. "Did you find her?"

"Nothing yet, Cathy, but I'm glad you're here. Teddy's coming over and..." With that, Teddy parked and bound up the front walk. She threw her arms around Cathy and gave her a good squeeze. I led them into the house and sat Cathy on the chair by the fire. I pointed at the logs and flicked a flame into being.

Cathy looked from the flame to me, surprise etching her face. I grabbed an afghan and spread it around her, tucking her into the chair. "I've never seen Penny perform any magic. She always said it was safer for me not to know..." Tears that had rimmed her red eyes fell to her cheeks. She sobbed. "What if...she's dead, Alex?" She croaked out the words. The hounds, still glamored, gathered at her feet and lay, lending their warmth and comfort.

"Don't even think it, Cathy. We'll find Penny. I promise."

"Alive...Alex? Do you...promise to find...her alive?" Cathy spoke with ragged breaths.

Gooseflesh coated my arms and shimmied down my body. I wasn't sure if that meant yes, I would, or no, I wouldn't, but I couldn't think of that now. "I promise, Cathy. Teddy and I are going to scry to find her."

"What's 'scry' mean?" She asked. Of course, she wouldn't know. How could she? Her relationship with Penny was strictly need-to-know, and as a non-mage, Cathy wouldn't have been exposed to witchy ways.

"It's a way to locate someone missing. Penny uses a pendulum. So do I, but also a mirror or crystal ball."

"Sounds...impossible." Cathy shook her head.

I kneeled in front of her and the hounds, so I could look her in the eye. "It's not impossible, Cath. It does work, and it's the only way I know to help us find Penny. Do you want to watch?" Cathy nodded. "Teddy, in that armoire is a map of Dagon County and my crystal ball. Can you grab them and put them on the dining room table?

"On it, boss." Teddy's usual cheerful demeanor and colorful language were toned down, her face solemn. I couldn't imagine what she must be thinking, as a burgeoning witch. She wasn't natural born, but, after she came to Castle Point, on the run from her wannabe demon boyfriend—whom we exiled—she made the choice to study and become a witch like me. That choice came with potential consequences, but she knew the risks.

We all did.

Cathy stood and shed the blanket. The three of us—four with Blackjack—moved into the dining room. The hounds stayed nestled on the floor in front of the fire. Teddy spread the map out over the table. Blackjack jumped onto the table and sat on one corner of the map. I slipped my pendulum out of my pocket and handed it to her. It probably wasn't the right time, but, since we didn't have to scry for someone often—close to never—I thought it a good teaching moment.

"Hold the pendulum by the top of the chain and let the crystal dangle. That's it, but don't hold it too tightly," Teddy followed my instructions. "Now, lean over the map, holding your arm out over top. It's tricky to keep your arm still, but try." Teddy nodded. "Good. Now, we say the spell."

*"Goddesses of the North, East, South, and West, hear our plea,
grant our request.
Help us locate those lost to us now, and help us fulfill our
sacred vow,
to protect those who are in danger, help us find Penny now, not
never."*

THE PENDULUM MOVED. Teddy and Cathy sucked in a breath. I glanced at them both. Cathy's red-rimmed eyes were saucers, and Teddy's eyes danced with delight. The crystal started to swirl in large circles. I watched, expecting the pendulum to slow down, and swing tighter, directing us to Penny's location but it didn't. The circle went wider and wider.

Teddy glanced at me, arching one eyebrow. "Is it supposed to do this?"

I shook my head. "No, it should wind down, honing in on her location." I put out my hand. Teddy grabbed the crystal, stopped the swing, and handed it to me. I gave it a go.

The same thing happened when I tried. I stopped the pendulum and looked at Cathy.

Cathy's eyes met mine. "What does that mean, Alex?"

"It either means she's not in the county, or..." I couldn't bring myself to finish the sentence.

"Or what, Alex?" Cathy pressed.

I pursed my lips into a thin line. I wanted to tell her, but the words tasted bitter on my tongue, so I just shook my head.

"She's dead? Is that what it means?" Cathy threw her hands to her mouth and sobbed. I went to her, holding her, feeling her body quake and convulse until she somewhat settled. Teddy joined us in a group hug, where we stood for several minutes.

"We don't know that for sure, Cathy, so let's not think it, okay?" I held her by the shoulders. She nodded. "Just because the pendulum circled the map, it doesn't mean she's…" I broke off. "It could just mean she's not in Dagon County. I'm going to try scrying with my crystal ball. Hopefully, I'll be able to see Penny, wherever she is. Okay?" Cathy nodded again and took a shaky breath.

I sat at the dining room table. Teddy and Cathy each took a seat to watch. Blackjack lay on the table, his paws tucked up under his chest. I smoothed my hands over the energy of the crystal ball, not touching it. I said the location spell again as I worked my hands back and forth over the crystal's energy field. A cloudy shape started to form inside the crystal. I stopped moving my hands, resting them on my lap instead. I peered into the crystal, connecting my energy with the ball.

The house fell silent. My vision tunneled into the dark cloud within the ball, as if I had blinders on my eyes, my periphery no longer existed. I willed the crystal to show me Penny's location, but nothing appeared. I breathed deeply, focusing my intention and my vision deeper inside the ball for several minutes.

Nothing.

The dark gray cloud dissipated, as my focus disconnected. I leaned back in my chair.

Cathy touched my arm. "Alex? Did you see her? Do you know where she is?"

I turned to look at her, meeting her eyes. "Nothing, Cathy. I'm so sorry." She sobbed again.

My heartache was large and loud, my heart painfully

thudding inside my chest. I could only imagine what Cathy was feeling. If only...

Like a hard slap to the face, a thought occurred to me. I stood up, my chair skittering back.

Cressy.

TEN

ALEXANDRA

I assured Cathy that I had another plan, but needed time to work it out. I didn't think including her in the summoning process would be a good idea. She'd had enough magical insight for one day, so I asked if she'd like to take a nap, or just relax in the guest bedroom upstairs. Cathy, sleep deprived and worn out from all the crying, agreed and snuggled gratefully into the guest bed.

Teddy and I closed the heavy living room drapes, locked all the doors, and prepared the room for summoning Cressy. We rolled up the antique rug and pushed it aside, set up black candles in heavy, brass holders around a circle of salt, and lit a small cauldron, adding witch's hair, copaiba resin, silver sage, and a small square of fabric cut from one of Cressy's suits. Teddy danced around the living room, a wee Sprite, excited about learning something new. "I've never summoned anyone before! Is it super cool, or super scary?"

I smiled. "It's kinda both. Except, not scary where Cressy is concerned."

"How long has he been your mentor?"

"As long as I've been alive. Longer actually."

"Ooo, I wish I had a ghosty guy I could summon. I'd have him over all the time! Parrrrteeee!" Teddy wiggled her bottom and danced in a circle. I stifled my laughter, mindful of Cathy sleeping upstairs. I slid Cressy's Grimoire from its place on the living room bookshelf and opened it to the summoning spell. I had it memorized but needed Teddy to read it too. She did so, then closed her eyes, her lips moving, repeating it to herself.

"Ok, got it."

"Great, let's get started."

"Heaven to Earth, hear my plea, bring back he who watches over me.
Goddess and Gods of North, East, South, West,
allow me to commune with our dear Cress."

The swirl of cloudy smoke from the cauldron showed Cressy's arrival. Teddy's eyes grew as wide as her smile as she watched Cressy fully form inside the circle. His smoking jacket, slicked-back grey hair, and thin mustache completed his dapper look.

Cressy smiled. "Alexandra, my dear. To what do I owe this immense pleasure?" He noticed Teddy standing there, trying her hardest not to wiggle like an excited puppy. "Who have we here?"

"This is Theodora Cunningham, Master Herbalist of my apothecary." I pushed some salt aside so Cressy could exit the circle. He stepped out and reached for Teddy's hand. I thought her eyes couldn't bulge any larger. I was wrong.

"So lovely to meet you, my dear." Cressy raised her hand up to his lips and pressed a ghostly kiss on her tiny knuckles.

"Wowee. I could feel that!" She squealed. "Amazing! Do it again!"

Cressy laughed heartily, took Teddy by the shoulders, and landed a kiss on her cheek.

Teddy swooned. "You're so super sexy for an old, dead guy."

I smacked my hand to my forehead. Cressy laughed again, then turned to me. "She's an absolute delight, Alexandra. Where did you find her?"

"She was on the run from an idiot boyfriend who fancied himself a demon. I expelled him, hired Teddy, and have been teaching her my witchy ways." I smiled.

Cressy pulled me into a warm embrace. "So good to see you, my dear. Tell me, why have you summoned me? Do you need help with another demon?"

"Not this time, Cress. Penny is...missing."

"Missing? Oh, dear. Did you try a location spell?"

I nodded. "Yes, that's the first thing we tried, but... nothing."

"I see. So, you'd like me to have a look?"

"I was hoping you could go further. Maybe see if she's been taken out of Dagon County..." I gulped for air, "or see if she's...d-d-dead." The canal of tears threatening to fall gave way. Cressy held me close.

"Oh, my sweet child. Of course, I will look for you." He released me and stepped back into the circle. He took a ghostly breath and his apparition swirled into a cloudy, gray vortex. Teddy stood beside me, grabbed my hand, and stood, watching. After several minutes, the clouds gathered into full form once again. Cressy smiled. My heart leaped.

"You found her?"

He shook his head. "No, unfortunately. Something is blocking me from seeing her location, *but* I can tell you that she is certainly *alive*."

The breath I was holding came out in a 'whoop', my heart racing. Teddy danced around the room, cheering.

"Cressy, thank you. That's wonderful news."

He pressed a long, elegant finger to his lips. "Good news, yes. However, there's still the issue of *finding* her. Have you any clues at all?"

I shook my head. "No clues, no. Just a fear." My entire body vibrated with it.

"And what's that, my dear?"

"The Witch Hunters have her."

Cressy pursed his lips in a low whistle. "If that's the case, then we have to assume she's in the castle."

I nodded. "But why couldn't you see her there? Why couldn't we find her when we scried for her?"

"Excellent question, Alexandra. Why, indeed. A cloaking spell, perhaps?"

I nodded in agreement. "Has to be, Cressy."

Teddy piped up. "You think there's a cloaking spell over the castle? Would that keep us from entering?"

"No." I said, "Guards around Penny would do that... and security cameras. Although, last time I was there, I only saw cameras around the outside of the building, not the inside... and—"

Teddy finished my thought. "And if we were glamored as Witch Hunters, we'd fit right in!"

"Exactly." I agreed, looking at Cressy.

"Excellent plan, albeit dangerous. Be careful, my dears." Cressy tucked a long finger under my chin. I nodded and lifted my hands towards Cressy, then Teddy.

High fives, all around.

I skimmed through the plan in my mind. A couple of speed bumps had me questioning our plan—such as whether the Witch Hunters had a spell on the castle so our glamor wouldn't work—but pushed it aside for now.

The important part was that Penny was alive.

We said goodbye to Cressy as his apparition faded.

I ran to the guest room and quietly opened the door. Cathy was sound asleep, snoring lightly. I let her be for now, although I couldn't wait to tell her the good news.

ELEVEN

ALEXANDRA

A knock on the door startled me as I walked down the stairs to join Teddy in the living room. The security camera experts had arrived. After a brief chat about where the cameras should be installed, they went straight to work. Cathy woke up and came downstairs.

Teddy and I were waiting, looking up at her. She stopped mid-step.

"What's going on?" She asked, tentatively.

"We have good news, Cath," I said.

Her eyes grew wide. "You found her? Where is she?"

Dammit. I shook my head. "No, we didn't find her, but we know she's *alive*."

Cathy took the remaining steps in a rush and flew into my arms. Teddy giggled, rubbing Cathy's back. "Oh, Alex, that's such good news! How did you...? Never mind, I don't need to know," she pulled back from the embrace and smiled. Her eyes were still puffy and red, and salty tear tracks dried on her cheeks.

The three of us moved into the kitchen for a small bite to eat and a pot of tea.

"I should probably go, and let you do...whatever it is you plan to do now..."

"Nonsense, Cathy. I insist you stay with me until we find Penny and bring her home."

"But what if she comes home and I'm not there?" Her voice was small, almost childlike.

"Do you have your cell on you?" Cathy nodded. "Then I'm sure she'll call. Seriously, Cathy. You shouldn't be alone. I have plenty of guest rooms. I even have spare toothbrushes and a pair of pajamas you can borrow." I didn't bother to mention that I had bought clean toothbrushes in the event I had a late-night sleepover with...a *man*.

The toothbrushes remained sealed in their packages.

So, that should tell you something.

Cathy agreed. The security installer knocked on the kitchen door. He and his crew came inside to install the monitors and show me how to use them. Cathy and Penny took their tea into the living room and chatted while I got the security business out of the way. The system seemed user-friendly. A larger monitor was set up in the kitchen. When connected, I could change the views to one camera at a time, or all the cameras around the house. I set it for all the cameras. A smaller monitor worked on Bluetooth, so I could take it with me throughout the house, or up to my room at night.

Perfect.

The protection jars, along with the security system, should be more than enough to keep the vandals—or anything that planned to do us harm—away.

Teddy invited herself to sleep over too, and why not? I had enough rooms. She and Cathy had agreed, Teddy would slip home for a few things, and then over to Cathy's gathering some personal items and her phone charger, and be back soon. When she had, it was quite late. None of us felt like eating a big dinner, so we nibbled on snacks, sipped wine, and chatted.

Cathy was the first to yawn. "I think I may actually sleep, Alex. Thank you for everything."

"You're more than welcome, Cathy. Please rest easy, ok? We will find her. I promise." Cathy's eyes dropped to the floor, but she nodded. I showed Teddy to the downstairs guest room, gave her a couple of towels, and said goodnight.

I walked with heavy, tired footsteps upstairs. I hardly had the energy to brush my teeth, but I did, then set the small Bluetooth monitor on the night table, stripped, and flopped onto my bed in a heap, Blackjack joining me.

I can't say how long I was out before I heard a soft beeping coming from the monitor. The beeping got increasingly louder as I came out of my slumber. When I realized what the sound was, I was suddenly and fully awake.

Grabbing the monitor, I hit the silence button and peered at it. Light and dark gray images appeared on the screen. I squinted, holding it closer to my face, then closing one eye. Sleep grated on my eyeballs. I rubbed my eyes and tried again.

I could hardly believe what I was seeing but didn't want to turn on the bedside lamp, not yet anyway, for fear of the perpetrator seeing and rushing away. There was nobody in the yard, but there was a lineup of people in what looked like dark robes along both sides of the backyard. They were spaced out along the edge of my property. Sleep halted my brain from thinking clearly. Why weren't they coming into the yard?

Then it hit me.

The protection jars.

Whatever, or whoever was skirting the property, *couldn't step inside.*

I crept out of bed and went to my window, but it was perched too high over the house, and I couldn't get a good view of the backyard, so I snuck downstairs, mindful of the creaky parts of the staircase. I tiptoed passed Teddy's room to the kitchen.

Dammit. I hadn't closed the curtains.

Moonlight slipped through, spreading a low glow on the tile floor. I got down on all fours and crawled over to the monitor on the kitchen counter. I worked the controls on the monitor, flicking first from all cameras to one at a time. Taking a moment to be impressed with the high-tech equipment, I zoomed in on a couple of the dark figures.

They wore dark robes that covered their heads. I'd seen something like this before, in the castle, when I was sneaking around looking for a damn important book, but this wasn't quite the same. Zooming in closer to one figure, I saw a white band across the top of the hood and a large, white, circular collar across the chest.

Was that...a...nun?

I peered closer, zooming the camera in as far as it would go, unable to believe what I was seeing. I crept to the window, and, staying low, peered outside. From this vantage point, I could see a line of nuns, at least an arm's length apart if not more, wearing habits, their white crown bands, and wimples glowing in the crescent moonlight.

I could see a glimmer of moonlight bouncing off the large silver crosses on chains around their necks. The nuns were mesmerized, looking straight ahead, into the yard, but not speaking. Their hands were tucked into their tunics.

The dark-robed figures Penny chased the other night! This must be them. Kids dressed up like nuns.

For the love of the Goddess.

I stood up. The kitchen was dark, except for the moonlight, which wasn't enough to call attention to me. I stepped to the back door and slowly opened it, waiting for the soft click of release before swinging it open and slipping outside.

I got to the top porch step and looked from side to side. I was about to yell at them to get the hell away from my yard but stopped. The nuns flanked either side of the yard, but no one along the cliff edge. Made sense, I guessed. The protection jars were on the furthest corners of the property, so bypassing them to walk along the edge would be tricky.

My brow furrowed, peering into the dimly lit night.

Why were they just standing there?

I reached for my earring and tugged.

The protection jars.

They protected the property from evil or demonic presence. Any innocent would easily be able to bypass them and come to the door, just like the security workers had earlier.

Which meant the nuns—or whoever wore the costumes—were *demonic*.

The moment I thought about it, sucking in a sharp breath, the nuns turned their heads toward me, in unison. They saw me standing on the porch and...snarled. Bearing razor-sharp teeth, their eyes a bright red, glowing like small red beams of light, directed at me.

Definitely not a bunch of punks in costume.

But not nuns, either.

A light flicked on in the kitchen. I turned to see Teddy

padding her way to the door. "Alex? What's going on? Why are you up?"

"Teddy, shhh!" She put a hand to her mouth but joined me on the porch.

When I turned to point out the nuns...they were gone.

CHAPTER

TWELVE

ALEXANDRA

E arl Dagon had his arm wrapped around Penny's throat, a knife clasped in his other hand. Penny reached for me, unable to scream, her face growing red, her breath coming in spurts from behind the Earl's firm grasp.

Several nuns crept toward the Earl and Penny, teeth bared. Blood dripped from their jagged edges. Their faces were nearly as white as the collars they wore, eyes rimmed black, pupils glowing red. I tried to reach for Penny, but my feet were cemented to the ground, my hands reaching through heavy iron bars.

We were in the castle dungeon.

The scene flipped. Penny was on the pyre. The nuns and Witch Hunters surrounded her, the hunters holding torches, the nuns dancing around the pyre, decorating it in toilet paper. They finished when the hunters lowered the torches to the base of the pyre. The dry wood and paper ignited instantly. Flames licked Penny's body and her copper-red hair.

She screamed and screamed.

I could feel the heat of the flame. Sweat dripped down my

temples, neck, and back. I tried to move toward her, but the Earl held me back. He wrapped his arm around my waist, then my throat. His raspy voice coated my mind; "You're next."

I was shaking and screaming, trying to escape, screaming for Penny...helpless as I watched my best friend engulfed in a fiery fury...

"Alex! Alex, wake up!" Teddy and Cathy were shaking me. My eyes flew open, breaths coming in gasps.

Another dream about Earl Dagon.

And the Witch Hunters.

And also the weird-ass nuns.

This was getting ridiculous.

"I'm awake." I laid back in my sweat-soaked sheets and closed my eyes, willing the shakes to subside.

"Another dream, Alex?" Teddy asked, curling up beside me. Cathy joined us from the other side. I looked from one to another, momentarily wondering how and why there were there, then I remembered. They slept over.

And Penny was alive.

"Yes. A terrible one, actually."

"About Penny?" Cathy asked in a small voice.

I turned to look her in her doe eyes. "Yes. But I think the dream was trying to confirm what I already guessed."

"Ooh! What's that?" Teddy asked, sitting up.

"That she's in the dungeon of Castle Dagon."

"What? Why? How?" Cathy and Teddy asked in unison.

"And also, who put her there?" Teddy asked.

I gathered my strength and sat up. "A lot of questions without coffee, ladies. I have something important to tell you, though. Let's make some and I'll explain..."

THIRTEEN

ALEXANDRA

"Blake is a Witch Hunter?" Teddy asked

"Blake knows Penny's a witch?" Cathy asked at the same time.

I nodded my head. "Yes, on both counts." I had just finished telling them everything Blake had told me the day before.

Teddy shook her head. "That smarmy rat-booger. I oughta sic the hounds on him." Hearing Teddy, the hounds lumbered into the kitchen. She kneeled to greet them. "Wanna eat deputy for snack time, babies? Hmm?" The hounds' long tongues lapped at her.

I glanced at Cathy. Tears were streaming down her face. "Oh, Cathy. I'm so sorry. I shouldn't have told you all that... I..."

"No, it's okay Alex. I'm glad you've told me as much as you have. I knew the risks Penny faced being a witch, but I never wanted to believe what the folklore said. I married Penny because I love her, and being a witch is who she is. I'm prepared to face an eventuality that..." she paused, sobs caught in her throat. I wrapped my arms around her.

"Don't go there, Cathy. We'll find her. And we know she's alive, so that's something. We just need to be smart and stay sharp and..."

I looked past Cathy at the kitchen door. Blake stood, looking through the window. He smiled sheepishly and knocked softly. I pulled away from Cathy and opened the door. Blake stepped inside. The minute he did, Cathy launched herself at him, pounding his chest with her small fists.

"You took her, you bastard! Bring her back! Bring back my wife!"

Blake grasped her fists and held firm. "Cathy, I promise you, I didn't take Penny, and I don't know where she is—I..." He stopped short as the hounds came close, growling a deep, throaty growl. They circled him, sniffing, growling, drool spilling from their flappy Mastiff lips, and pooling on the floor. I shot Teddy a look. She was gleefully tapping her fingers together.

"Teddy, call them off, please," I asked. She did. The hounds took their place on either side of her and sat at the ready.

"Thanks," Blake said in a hushed tone. Cathy whipped her hands away from him and sat on a kitchen chair, wiping at her eyes and nose with a tissue.

"Blake, what are you doing here?" I asked.

"I didn't like the way we left things yesterday...I... wanted to apologize —again—and let you know that I'm trying to find Penny."

"I thought I clarified that I don't want your help."

He glanced down, rubbing a spot on the kitchen floor

with the toe of his boot. "I know you did, and I understand, but I really want to help. I feel responsible."

"You are responsible!" the three of us yelled, and the hounds growled again. Blake backed up a step, eyes wide.

"Okay, yes, I know! But, now I want to help..." he added, running his hand through his hair.

A waft of lavender mint tickled my senses. I closed my eyes briefly, then snapped them open again.

"Blake, what makes you think we could trust you now?"

He eyed me warily. "You just...can."

I narrowed my eyes at him. Teddy and Cathy glanced from me to Blake and back to me. I let out a huff of air.

"What's the plan?"

FOURTEEN

BLAKE

The look in Alexandra's eyes devastated me. I knew I shouldn't care about what she thought, but I did. The hollow pit in my stomach ached. It was there, partly from not eating since seeing Alex at the station, to feeling bad for Penny.

"What's the plan?" Alex asked.

Good question.

Meeting her eyes, then Cathy's and Teddy's, I briefly wondered if they were witches as well. I shook it off. I couldn't imagine what Alexandra would do to me if I started poking around. Penny missing was bad enough.

"I'll have to see what I can find out at the next meeting."

"The Witch Hunter meeting?" Alex asked.

I shuffled my feet. "Yeah."

"When is it?" She narrowed her eyes at me.

"Why?"

She paused. "Gee, Blake. What reason could I possibly have for asking? *Penny's missing*, remember? The sooner we find her, the sooner we can get her out of whatever prison she's being held at."

"We don't know for sure that another hunter took her, Alex."

"Who else could it be?"

"Anyone! Point is, until I find out more, we shouldn't assume."

Alexandra crossed her arms in front of her magnificent chest and stepped closer to me. The scent of her rose perfume hit me hard. She looked up at me, her deep green eyes piercing what was left of my soul.

"They have her, Blake. We *have to* assume."

I nodded my head. "Okay, fine. I'll see what I can find out. There's a meeting tomorrow evening at the castle."

"We'll be there." All three of the ladies spoke in unison.

"What? No, that's ludicrous. What are you thinking?"

Alex spoke up. "We'll be there, Blake, just...hiding."

I peered at her. "Then you should know that they've upgraded the security system since..." I stopped. "Someone broke in a few weeks ago."

Alex uncrossed her arms. "What did they do? To upgrade it, I mean."

"Installed more security cameras, outside, and inside, too."

Alex tapped a finger against her full lips, then tugged at her earring. "Not an issue." She stated flatly.

I quirked a brow. "Not an issue? What does that mean?" I looked from Alex to Teddy and Cathy.

All three of them just stared back at me, lips pressed into thin lines.

Got it.

Witchy stuff.

Made me wonder what kind of witchy stuff they could

do to keep from being spotted on the security cameras. I also wondered if Penny had the same powers and if she was taken by a Witch Hunter, who would be the one to take those powers from her...

The aching pit in my stomach flared.

FIFTEEN

BLAKE

I parked, stepped out of my car, and slipped on my cloak. Despite the warmth of the woolen cloak, I shivered. Glancing around the parking lot, I looked for Alex and her crew. Not seeing them, I entered Castle Dagon under another cloak—of darkness. Meetings always took place after dark, and tonight, the moon took refuge behind the robust October clouds. Although it wasn't a secret that the Witch Hunters existed in the world, the Order liked to assume some anonymity of the hunters, so meetings were held after dark, and the parking lot was protected by a tall fence and shrubs, so our cars weren't obvious to any passerby.

When I stepped inside, I looked for Alex again and shook my head. Did I really think they'd risk being here? The idea was ludicrous. They'd be arrested for trespassing after museum hours. Or worse, they'd risk exposing themselves as witches and be thrown in the dungeon to await their fate.

Assuming they were all witches, that is.

And would do something stupid to expose themselves.

I flashed to the time Alex saved me from a demon by throwing an 'energy ball' his way and shuddered. I supposed she could do some pretty awesome damage to the hunters if she really wanted to.

If she was backed into a corner, for instance.

Or determined to get Penny back.

I hoped to be far away from her wrath if that ever happened. Maybe tuck in behind another hunter. Maybe the hunter who took Penny to begin with, if it was a hunter who did.

Use him as a shield.

I smirked and tossed the large hood over my head and slipped into the courtyard, taking my place in the circle of hunters, and began chanting praise to the Earl Dagon and Demon Vine in the ancient language of the hunters. Peering around the circle from under the protection of my hood, a coldness settled in my belly. It had to be a hunter who took her. I had admitted to Penny being a witch at a previous meeting, there were only so many people named Penny in Castle Point, so it was only a matter of time before someone figured it out. I wondered who would confess to the crime.

Wait...*was it a crime?*

Witchcraft had been illegal for over 400 years since Earl Dagon implemented the law and created the Order of the Witch Hunters, so really...I couldn't even call it kidnapping.

It was more like stealing *my prize.*

I was the one who exposed Penny. She should be my kill, and her powers should be mine.

My stomach squirmed, bile swiftly rising into my throat. I choked it down. The faint scent of roses hit and I peered around the room again. *Was Alex here?* All I could see were large men in woolen robes, faces covered by huge hoods. I sniffed the air. Nothing. *My imagination playing tricks.* Alex would do nothing as crazy as being anywhere near the Order.

The High Commander entered the courtyard and took his place on the far side of the circle. Inside the circle, the pyre of sticks and branches sat waiting for a witch to lie on them. The branches were old and well-weathered from years of exposure to the elements by the open ceiling. They were kept in place for the benefit of the museum tours, but, one day soon, would finally fulfill their purpose and be replaced by new ones.

If Penny was taken by a hunter, that is.

Not a big 'if.'

The High Commander raised his staff, silencing our chant.

"It has come to my attention that the witch known as Penny has been taken and is now sequestered in the castle dungeon." Audible gasps flowed through the room.

What the hell?

Sheriff Roberts, the High Commander, told me he did not know who took Penny or where she was. Was he lying? Or maybe he found out just before the meeting?

He continued, "Would the successful hunter please step forward so that you may be rewarded."

I raised my head. Something we were never to do in the Commander's presence, but I wanted to see who kidnapped Alexandra's friend.

No, I mean...*stealing my prize.*

No, I mean, *kidnapping Alex's friend.*

A good nurse. An innocent, lovely wife and friend.

A witch. An evil, murderous, untrustworthy adversary.

My head pounded.

I snapped back to the room as one hunter pulled away from the circle and took a knee before the High Commander. The robes and hood protected his face. I couldn't see who it was. I had to hold my feet in place to keep from running over and yanking his hood off.

"It was I who took the witch, your Honor."

"Very good, hunter. Although, I believe it was another hunter who exposed the witch, to begin with, your successful capture is admirable."

"Thank you, Commander. I, along with many of my fellow hunters, grew impatient, sir, and so I took the liberty of the capture."

The entire circle of hunters, aside from maybe two, turned their hooded heads my way. I felt a flush of heat through my torso and head and bowed my head further.

"You've done well, hunter. I congratulate you on your successful capture. We will proceed with the stripping ceremony on the eve before Hallows, and celebrate with a feast and wine around the burning pyre on Hallow's Eve!"

A cheer rose from the circle of hunters, fists thrown high in the air.

Except for two.

The same two who refused to look my way earlier.

They stood, stoic and unmoved.

I wished I could see who they were and wondered why they weren't celebrating with the rest of them. Maybe they had got close to capture as well, but were too late? That must be it. Not that it mattered. Penny had been captured and was being held here in the castle dungeon, awaiting her fate.

As the meeting broke up and the hunters left, congratulatory slapping the successful hunter on the back. I followed for a few steps, hoping the hunter would pull off his hood and reveal himself, but he didn't. I could follow him out to his car but took a detour. Just as I was about to head for the dungeon stairs, the High Commander called me.

"Hunter! Come here."

"Yes, Commander." I turned and took a knee before Sheriff Roberts.

"You should know that we have confirmation of another witch."

My breath caught. "Who, may I ask, Commander?"

"Alexandra Heale."

My stomach roiled. Hot bile rose high in my throat and I coughed.

The High Commander's voice dropped. "I know you know, Blake. You had to have known. Penny and Alexandra are friends and you've been getting very close to Alexandra as of late."

I stood up, nodding. "Yes, Commander."

That was it, then. I would have to bring Alex in. I'd have to strip her powers and burn her at the pyre. If I didn't, someone else would. At least I would treat her with some form of dignity. I couldn't imagine another hunter doing the same.

"I will bring her in, Gordon." Tossing the formalities aside, I stood up and lowered my hood, meeting Gordon's eyes. He kept his hood in place but raised it enough to look me in the eyes.

"That can't happen, Blake."

"Excuse me, sir?"

"Alexandra Heale is untouchable."

Untouchable? What did that mean? I didn't know whether to jump for joy or laugh. I focused on keeping my face neutral. "What does that mean, sir?"

"Blake, we've known Alexandra Heale is a witch since... well, since she was born, actually."

This was news.

So, all my attempts at keeping her secrets were futile. The hunters already knew.

"I'm confused, sir. If the hunters knew, why wasn't she burned...as a child?"

"The command to leave Alexandra alone comes from Earl Dagon himself."

I shook my head. Frowning at the Sheriff. "Excuse me, sir? How's that possible? The Earl has been dead for... centuries."

Gordon nodded. "That's true. However, Alexandra is the Earl's last remaining blood ancestor *and* the reincarnation of the Earl's Evelyn. *She's Evelyn of Cumbria.*"

The room spun. I blew out the breath I had been holding, bent over, and clasped my hands to my knees.

Alex is Evelyn? The Evelyn? The evil witch who spurned the Earl and was the reason for the law, the Order, and the world's history?

"You're certain, sir?"

"Yes, absolutely. It's even recorded in the 'Book of the Hunters'," the Commander nodded toward a door further down the hallway. He was referring to the oldest book in the castle, hidden in plain sight, under glass in the castle library. I had learned the ancient language as a child but had no clue that the woman they spoke of was Alexandra.

My Alexandra.

"Does she know, sir?"

Gordon shook his head. "We don't believe so, no. She was well protected by her mentor, Waldo Cress. Although we could never prove that Mr. Cress was a witch himself, so he was never captured."

I nodded my head, chewing on my bottom lip.

"So, she can't be touched? By the hunters, I mean?" I hoped the dimly lit corridor would hide the relief on my face.

"Correct. However…" Gordon paused. "There is a plan underway. Not by the hunters, but by Earl Dagon himself. She will soon be delivered to Dagon by burning on the pyre to rejoin him and his wife, Madeline, on his throne. I believe this will happen on Hallow's Eve."

Chills ripped through me. "What? Why? *How?*"

"The Earl has sent his sentries, commanded by their leader, Madeline Bavant—the Earl's wife—to do the task."

Panic rose with the bile in my throat. "His sentries? Who are they, sir?"

"We aren't actually sure. We must leave it up to Earl Dagon to complete the task and be rejoined with his Evelyn once again." Gordon turned to leave, then turned back. "Be clear about this, Blake; you are not to interfere in the Earl's command. Is that understood?"

I nodded my head. "Perfectly, sir."

"And stay away from the dungeon." He nodded in the direction I had been heading. "The dungeon is protected by Dagon's magic, but we don't want any of the hunters taking a chance. The witch down there is a fiery red-headed devil." He patted his chest. "I have the skeleton key and am in charge of the prisoner. Understood?"

"Perfectly, sir."

The Sheriff turned and walked toward the door.

Slamming my hand against my mouth, I reached for the nearest vase and hurled.

CHAPTER
SIXTEEN

ALEXANDRA

Teddy, Blackjack, and I waited under the cover of bushes and the absent moon outside the castle for the other hunters to arrive. We watched Blake get out of his car, don his cloak, and head inside the building.

"Ok, Teddy, let's do this."

Teddy was in charge of the glamor. She pulled out her wand and swirled. Like Cinderella's fairy godmother, my appearance changed from top down into that of a Witch Hunter. Teddy did the same to herself, then turned the wand to Blackjack.

"Wait, what is she doing?" His silky voice purred through my mind.

"Just let her, Blackjack. It's for your protection."

"Geez, woman. A little head's up would have been nice." He whined as Teddy's wand completed the glamor, turning Blackjack into a little house mouse.

"Oh, now this is humiliating!" he peered up at us with beady red eyes.

I giggled and whispered. "You look adorable, Blackjack. Now, let's go!"

We stepped out of the darkness and stepped in behind the last of the hunters entering the castle. With the hoods covering our faces, we easily blended into the throng. And why wouldn't we? We looked exactly like them. The only thing that stayed the same was the color of our eyes. Regardless, we kept to the back of the line. I glanced up and around the large entryway. Sure enough, Blake was right. Interior security cameras had been installed recently.

Thank the Goddess for glamor.

Blackjack slipped under the door and skittered across the floor, easily hiding among the antiques lining the corridor to the courtyard. When we turned the corner, I stopped. Teddy bashed into me. The other hunters moved into the courtyard and formed a circle.

"Hey!" she whispered.

"Sorry. I just..." I looked up at the massive painting of Evelyn of Cumbria. Teddy followed the angle of my head and gasped.

"Holy Mother Goddess—*that's you!*" She whispered harshly.

"Shhh! No, it's not, but...it's weird, right?"

"I'd bet my best big boots it's you. The resemblance is super crazy uncanny," she replied before we settled into the back of the courtyard and took our place in the circle. Blackjack the mouse scooted under my robes and sat on the toe of my boot. The other hunters shuffled to make room for us but maintained their chanting.

Crap, the chants!

I reached for Teddy's hand and gave it a squeeze. One eye peered at me from under the hood, and she gave a little shrug. We chanted. Or rather, made a low-throated sound like chanting. None of the other hunters seemed to take notice, so we kept going. I peered around the circle and spotted Blake to my right, a few feet away. The only part of him I could see from under his cloak was his mouth and chin.

They were unmistakably his.

I'd recognize that chiseled jaw anywhere.

I pushed the prickling heat at the base of my belly away. No time for a hot cop fantasy. I saw him glance around and dropped my head.

The High Commander entered, silenced the men, and announced that Penny had been taken by a hunter and was being held in the castle dungeon! Teddy squeezed my hand hard, and I squeezed back. Shivers roiled through me. It took every ounce of energy to stay in place and not run down to the dungeon. That wouldn't have worked out so well for us. Every hunter would've been on us in a heartbeat.

Not that I couldn't energy-ball their asses back to the hell they were born from. Heat pushed through my hands, but not the good kind. The red-hot-piercing Dagon ancestral heat squirmed its way through my veins and rested in my hands, ready to take action.

"Harm Thee None, Alexandra." Cressy's voice floated through my mind.

Right. I'm a good witch, despite the evil blood running through my veins.

Why was it so hard to remember that?

Because I was in a circle of Witch Hunters.

The bane of all witches' existence, that's why.

The High Commander summoned the 'successful'

hunter to step forward. I glanced at Blake again. He stood solid, peering out from under his hood. Movement from my left caught my attention. Another hunter kneeled in front of the High Commander.

It wasn't Blake!

He was telling the truth!

He had nothing to do with Penny's disappearance. Aside from the nasty business of exposing her to the Witch Hunters in the first place, that is.

Something I could never forgive him for.

Knowing he hadn't taken Penny himself though, that was...something. I glanced around as an excited murmur rippled through the courtyard. The hooded hunter was a superhero among these men. There were no known witch captures in the world in the last fifty years, at least. We had gotten more and more clever in our practices. With the advancement of technology, it was even easier to communicate and remain 'underground.'

But who was the hunter? I carefully peered out from under my hood, hoping he would slip his off and reveal his identity, but no luck. They really took this cloaking thing seriously. Unless they'd head to the parking lot and get into their vehicles. I'd love to be there to see this asshole uncloaked, but Penny was the priority. I'd have to ask Blake later.

But then, I'd have to admit to Blake that I was here. Although I'd already told him we would be, I didn't tell him *how*. I'm sure he thought we were merely hiding in a corner somewhere, not glamored as a hunter. I was sure he'd have my hide for being this...*ballsy*.

Not that I cared. I would actually enjoy seeing the look on his face if I walked up to him and said 'boo'." I stifled a giggle.

The High Commander ended the meeting, and the circle of cloaks disbursed. Teddy and I followed, but not too closely. Many of the men walked alongside the victorious hunter, swatting him on the back and laughing. Still, no hoods shed.

Teddy grabbed my arm and shuffled me toward a dark part of the hall. Blake was doubling back, heading toward the stairs. The dungeon, perhaps? We watched as the High Commander summoned him. Blake kneeled, then rose and removed his hood. His handsome features glowed in the dim candle-lit hall and the stirring deep inside my belly returned. The High Commander kept his hood in place.

Dammit. I really wanted to know who the nasty bastard was.

We watched as the men spoke in low, indiscernible tones. For a moment, Blake's features went white. "Can you hear what they're saying?" I mouthed. Teddy shook her head. After another few minutes, the High Commander left the hall, and Blake launched himself at the nearest urn and...vomited.

What the hell were they talking about that would make him want to blow chunks?

Blake wiped his mouth, tossed his hood back on his head, and headed for the stairs.

"Should we go down there?" Teddy whispered.

"Not yet. Let's just wait until he leaves. Then we'll check it out." Blackjack the mouse stepped off my boot and peered up at me.

"I'll run reconnaissance, woman."

"Great idea, mousy. Just don't get caught, and for Goddess' sake, don't step on any mousetraps."

Blackjack scurried off after Blake. Teddy and I waited, tucked behind the suit of armor across from the painting of

Evelyn of Cumbria. I stared at the painting and shuddered. It really looked like me, but thankfully, wasn't.

Cressy and I had worked through all of my past lives when I was a child, and Evelyn wasn't one of them. I could thank the Goddess for that. I mean, if I *was* Evelyn, that would mean that I'm responsible for Earl Dagons' law and the fate of the witch-kind for the past 400 years. Knowing that she was me would be a fate worse than what the Hunters put us through for centuries.

I couldn't live with that.

Teddy clung to my arm as the sound of heavy footsteps came from the stairwell. Blake appeared, his head still cloaked. He pulled off his hood. His face was solemn. *Had he talked to Penny?* Blackjack skittered toward us.

I whispered; "What did you see?"

"She's down there. The red-haired one. She's in a cell."

"Did you talk to her?"

Blackjack eyed me and shook his tiny, mousy head. *"No, silly woman. She can't hear me, remember?"*

"Oh, right."

"Did he?" Teddy asked, eyes wide.

"No, Penny can't hear the 'animal speak'," I whispered. "Blackjack, are there any guards near her cell?"

"Yes, but only one at the base of the stairs, in a vestibule just outside the cell-room door. The man and the guard exchanged a few words, but that was it. I couldn't see the red-haired one."

"Then how do you know she's down there if you didn't see her?"

"Geez, woman, what do you take me for-a dog? I heard the men speak. She's in the room past the vestibule in a cell."

Knots tied and untied themselves in my belly. I pulled at my earring. "Okay, let's go. Blackjack, lead the way." I grabbed Teddy's hand, and we moved toward the dark stairwell. Blackjack stopped at the top of the stairs. *"Wait here. I have an idea."*

Teddy and I tucked into the darkness of the hall beside the staircase and waited.

After a moment, we heard the piercing shriek of a tiny mouse. We gasped. *Blackjack!* Then another shriek. This time, the voice was deeper. *The guard!* Thunderous footsteps peeled up the staircase. The guard appeared, Blackjack the Mouse hot on his tail. The guard looked behind him and shrieked again, racing off toward the offices.

"Go! Now, woman!"

"Blackjack, you're brilliant! How'd you know he'd be afraid of mice?"

"I didn't! Just go!"

As quietly as our enormous boots could take us, we fled down the steps. The moment we reached the landing and entered the large room of cells, something shifted.

Teddy gasped, "The glamor!"

I looked down at myself. The Witch Hunter glamor had completely disappeared.

Mother Goddess!

"What's going on?" Teddy grabbed my arm with shaky hands.

"I don't know, but let's keep going!"

We raced into the room. The perimeter was all cells, replete with black bars. *"Penny!"* I whispered, harsh, but loud enough that I hoped she could hear.

She did.

Penny appeared, her face pressed up against the bars of a cell, toward the back of the large room.

"Alex! Teddy! Oh, thank the Goddess, you found me!"

"Shhhh! The guard is still here, upstairs. Blackjack has him cornered."

The moment I said it, we heard another shriek, then the sound of things breaking. "I'll get you, you diseas-infested rodent!" Blackjack was keeping the guard busy.

I grabbed Penny's arms through the cell bars and hugged her the best I could. Teddy did the same.

"Penny, are you okay?"

"Am I okay? Are you seriously asking me that right now? Do I look okay? Just get me the hell out of here!" She shook her long, curly head and anchored her hands on her hips.

Studying the cell door, I focused my intention on the lock. It looked as old as the castle itself, and likely needed a skeleton key to open it. I narrowed my eyes, then closed them, intending for the tumblers to turn.

Nothing happened.

I opened my eyes again and looked at the lock. "Ladies, help me out here. Let's work together."

"I've been trying, Alex, but I can't make it budge," Penny whispered, hands clasping the cell bars.

"Maybe with the three of us..."

Teddy perked up. "Worth a shot! Let's do it!"

Penny blew out the breath she had been holding, shook her hands out, clasped them together and snapped her knuckles, and rolled her neck around, cracking it. I shook the grin at my goofy friend off my face and peered at the lock again. Penny and Teddy did the same. We intended the heck out of the thing, but it wouldn't budge.

"What's going on?" I asked.

Teddy snapped her fingers. "For the love of Scooby-Doo, the place is under a protection spell!"

Penny and I snapped our heads toward her.

"What you mean, Scrappy-Doo?" Penny asked.

"The glamor! As soon as we reached the cell room door,

the glamor wore off, and now, we can't unlock the old-timey lock!"

I pulled at my earring. "Penny, have you tried your magic while you've been down here?"

Penny nodded, then bowed her head. "I thought it was because they'd already stripped me of my magic, but we hadn't done the stupid ceremony like the history books say, so I guess that's not the reason. I think Teddy's right. The dungeon is protected from magic."

Heat prickled the back of my neck and I took a deep breath. *The smarmy bastards.* Of *course,* they'd have thought to protect the dungeon. That's why we couldn't find Penny when we scryed for her. Even Cressy couldn't see past the dungeon's protective spell. It had to be protected because that's where they kept witches before...I stopped the thought. I didn't want to think about Penny's fate. I wouldn't *let* burning on the pyre *be* Penny's fate—I just couldn't.

I focused on my hands, willing an energy ball to appear. It didn't. I focused deeper, trying to conjure the evil Dagon blood to boil in my veins, but that didn't work either.

We were absolutely powerless here.

"Hey! What are you doing here?" The guard was back, his bulk taking up the doorway.

The three of us whipped around as he approached.

Teddy shrieked, grabbing my arm.

"Get out of here!" Penny shouted.

I froze. My feet wouldn't move as the guard came closer. My hands were icy cold. No hope for an energy ball there.

"Alex, we have to go!" Teddy pulled at my arm.

"Wait. I have an idea." If magic wouldn't work, perhaps something else would. I lifted my hand flat out to the guard. "Stop!"

He stopped.

I pointed one finger up. "Watch my finger." I waggled my finger back and forth. The guard's eyes followed my finger's path, back and forth, back and forth. "When I snap my fingers, you'll fall fast asleep, and forget we were ever here. One, two, three!" I snapped my fingers. The guard's head fell forward. Soft snoring ensued.

"What the heckin' heck, Alex? What did you just do?" Teddy asked, eyes wide.

"Hypnotized him."

"What?" Both girls asked.

"The power of suggestion, ladies. Lucky for us, I'm a hypnotist and he is highly suggestible." I walked closer to the guard.

"Can you make him cluck like a chicken? Bark like a dog? Oh, please, Alex..." Penny coaxed. I shook my head, smiling.

"I'd rather see if he has a skeleton key on him, Pen."

"Oh, yeah, that's a good idea. Sure, do that."

I checked his pockets. No key.

"Teddy, check around for a key hanging somewhere. I mean, there has to be a key, right?" I looked at Penny, her eyes filling with tears. She shook her head.

"No, Alex. I'm pretty sure the High Commander took the key. I heard him tell the night guard that he didn't trust that he won't fall asleep on his watch. He must have taken it, so I couldn't get my hands on it. Not that it would be easy," she tapped the bars.

Teddy threw her hands up. "What? But what if you have to tinkle?"

Penny pointed at a dark corner of the cell. "In Castle Dagon's history, they installed indoor plumbing in the dungeon." Teddy and I peered into the corner of the cell and saw the dim white of a ceramic toilet and a sink on the wall beside it.

"You've got to be kidding me. For the love of the Goddess," I breathed.

Penny smirked. "Yep. Chateau Dagon. Worst. Vacation. Ever."

I looked Penny in the eyes, my vision blurring with tears. "Oh, Pen. I'm so sorry! I don't know what else to do!" I grabbed her hands through the bars.

"It's okay Alex, thanks for trying." The three of us stood in silence for a moment, sniffing, light snores coming from the sleeping guard.

No. This wasn't the end. It couldn't be. I wouldn't let it.

"I'll figure out a way, Pen. I promise. We'll get you out."

Penny nodded, tears running down her face. "Tell Cath I love her, will you?" She choked.

"You'll be telling her yourself soon enough. I promise." I smiled through the wet, salty tears rolling down my cheeks.

"Don't make a promise you can't keep, Alex. Please."

"Don't tell me what I can and cannot do Pen."

She smiled through a stream of tears as we slipped past the sleeping guard, still standing in the middle of the hall. Once we stepped into the vestibule, Teddy -cast the glamor and we hoofed up the stairs, then sauntered nonchalantly toward the entry in case anyone was watching on the security cameras. Blackjack was waiting for us by the door.

"*A little heads up that the guard was coming would've been nice!*" I chided him.

"*I was a little busy trying to stay alive, woman. Did you find the red-haired one?*"

"*Yes, but the room is protected by magic. We can't get her out!*"

"*Well, you tried.*" Blackjack scurried under the door.

"*Nice, Blackjack.*" I frowned under the hooded cloak. "*If you aren't careful, I'll make sure you're a mouse for life.*"

"*Could be worse. I could be a witch in a cage.*"

He was right, I thought, as we walked through the parking lot and disappeared under the cover of darkness.

CHAPTER
SEVENTEEN

ALEXANDRA

Teddy and I dropped the glamor when we were far enough away from the castle security cameras to do so safely.

"What are you going to do, Alex? About Penny?" Teddy asked, her voice small and quiet.

I shook my head. "I don't really know, Teddy. But I have to think of something. I can't let them strip Penny's powers and burn her on the pyre. That much, I know."

But what could I do?

The castle was protected from magic. The dungeon anyway. And the Sheriff had the cell key.

Blake.

I'd have to remind him of his part in all this and of the time I saved him from a demon.

Time to call in a favor.

Why'd everything always come back to needing Blake?

I couldn't roll my eyes far enough, thinking about having to speak to the man again. Smell his damn Brut, lavender, and mint mix. Just the thought of it sent little jagged heat spikes into my belly.

Ugh.

Teddy and I hugged goodbye and went our separate ways. I strolled toward home, Blackjack, happy to be glamor-free, sticking close to my side. Cathy wouldn't be there. She headed home after the early morning visit from Blake, and I insisted the hounds go with her. Although Cathy didn't know the glamored hounds were from hell, she accepted the company gratefully, leashed the 'Bull Mastiffs,' and left.

The gloomy thick clouds covering the crescent moon matched the gloomy cloud covering my heart. I was relieved to find Penny but devastated that she was sequestered, alone, and afraid, in the castle dungeon.

Turning onto my street, I could see my house a half-block away. The gloomy clouds in my heart rained. As I stepped closer, a rustling from the neighbor's bushes caught my attention. A dark figure popped out of the bush. Then another, and another, and even more.

Witch Hunters?

My breath caught, and I froze in place, Blackjack beside me. I peered into the dark night as the figures approached. A glow of white around the figure's neck and head shined under the low glow of the street lamps.

"What the..." I heard Blackjack. *"Are they Witch Hunters, woman?"*

"Not Witch Hunters, Blackjack. *Nuns.*"

The nuns trotted toward us in unison, dagger teeth bared, red eyes blazing. We would not wait around to see if they wanted a fancy coffee. Blackjack and I bolted across the street toward my house. The nuns followed. Several rapid footsteps fell in behind me, getting closer. I risked glancing back over my shoulder. They were closing in.

"Go, Blackjack, *run*!"

We ran faster.

They followed faster.

I'd have to save the question of how a bunch of demonic nuns wearing floor-length habits could run as fast as me for later. Right now, I was too busy running for my life.

Blackjack got to the house before me and raced up to the top of the first tree. I got to the edge of my property, ran down the walkway, and was almost on the porch stairs when I realized they'd stopped. I hopped up on the porch and turned back, panting. Now spreading into a line of black-cloaked beings, the nuns stood on the sidewalk in front of the house.

They couldn't step foot on the property.

The protection jars!

I thanked the Goddess for her wisdom and recipes and pulled out my cell phone, punching Blake's number.

He picked up partway through the first ring.

"Alex? What's wrong?" Of course, he was awake. He'd left the castle not long before we did, and he likely wouldn't be able to sleep any more than I would, knowing Penny was locked in the dungeon below and was responsible.

"Blake, I think you better get over to my place. And bring your gun." I hung up and waited.

The nuns didn't move. They just sneered, their wretched sharp teeth bared at me, their eyes burning a hole in my soul. I watched as one of them tried to step forward but was thrown back the second its foot touched the property line.

Thank you, Goddess.

A few seconds later, the street was lit up with red and

blue flashing lights. No sirens. Blake was aware enough of the lateness of the night to wake up the entire neighborhood. He was fast. I briefly wondered if he had been sleeping in clothes.

Seeing the lights, the demonic nuns scattered, then clustered again and, hands tucked into their robes, hurried toward town.

Blake got out of his squad car as I jogged down the pathway and joined him.

"Alex? What's going on?"

"Shhhh, let's follow them and I'll explain!"

He lightly closed the car door and stepped beside me. We darted down the sidewalk, careful to duck behind cars if we saw any of the nuns turn their heads, but we didn't have to worry. They were on a mission—*no pun intended*—to get to where they were going.

"What's going on?" Blake whispered as we fast-paced toward the herd of black penguins.

"Remember the vandalism at my place and my business?" He nodded his head. "The other night, I saw these nuns surrounding my property. Only, they aren't really nuns."

Blake stopped. I stopped and turned toward him. "What?" I asked.

"Don't tell me..."

I forced a smile. "Ok, I won't tell you they're possessed by a demon—or demons."

He rolled his eyes and kept walking. "Seriously? How can you tell?" I rolled my eyes back at him. "Right, got it. Ok, so what's the plan here?"

"Well, if we follow them and find out where they're coming from, maybe I can figure out how to deal with them."

"Makes sense, I guess. But could be dangerous. You have magic, but you could use muscle."

I gave him a sideways glance. "That's why I invited you to the party, Blake."

"Oh. Right. Good thinking."

"I've said it before, and I'll say it again—good thing you're cute."

CHAPTER

EIGHTEEN

BLAKE

I couldn't sleep. My mind was reeling with the information High Commander Sheriff Gordon gave me earlier. When Alexandra called, at first I thought it was because her adorable witchy ears were burning, or she could hear my thoughts.

Or she was in trouble.

A blue streak of panic flushed through me when I answered the phone. I pulled my clothes on and was out the door within a hot minute.

Within *two* hot minutes, I'm crouching between cars and bushes, sneaking after a pack of nuns with Alex.

Life with that woman was anything but boring.

Except, I didn't *have* a life with that woman, and I honestly felt a little sad about that. Not that I should expect to. She was a witch and 'her kind' could never live with 'my kind.' It's just not possible.

Like Lex Luthor and Superman—enemies for life.

Gas and a flame, more like...get them together, and it's

an explosion and hot, burning fire.

That was actually more like how I felt about Alex. She's gas to my flame—well—the burning in my groin, in particular. I watched Alex quietly jogging and darting to avoid being seen by the nuns. The gloomy light reflected in waves of her long, black hair. The scent of her rose perfume wafted toward me with every fluff of her hair as she fast-paced along.

"Blake, look! The nuns are heading toward the church!"

Of course, they were. Where else would nuns go? I thought, but didn't want to state the obvious. We crouched and snuck over to the church, and waited behind some bushes as we watched the nuns go inside.

"Do you think Father Donovan knows he has a group of demonic nuns in his parish?" I asked.

Alexandra shrugged. "Honestly, all I know for certain is that the nuns are possessed and they're the ones responsible for the damage to my house and they just have to be the ones who tossed the eggs and spray painted my businesses," she spoke in low, hushed tones.

"Why would they do that? What do they have against... ohhhh." It hit me. The 'sentries' Gordon told me about earlier. The ones that Earl Dagon summoned to do his dirty work and capture Alex.

This had to be them.

I opened my mouth to tell Alex what I knew, but I was too late. She bolted out of the bushes and was already at the church door. "Alex, wait! Don't...!" But she opened the door and snuck inside, peering out at me and waving her hand at me to hurry and follow.

Taking a deep breath, I bolted to the door and fell in behind her, softly closing the door.

The church vestibule was littered with candles, the soft

glow casting eerie shadows on the walls. The stoup—holy water vessel—was just off to one side. I dipped my fingers in the water and crossed myself, then glanced at Alex, motioning her to do the same. She rolled her eyes at me and shook her head.

She slipped past me and peered into the nave. I folded my body on top of hers and peered in over her head. The scent of her shampoo and the rose perfume filled my nostrils, and I breathed deeply. Alex twisted her head around and peered up at me, eyebrows arched. I smiled and backed off. Good idea. My body parts were about to announce that they found her body parts super exciting.

The nuns were clustered near the pupil, on their knees. I counted eighteen nuns in all. They began chanting. My ears strained to hear them clearly, and a shiver ripped through me when I recognized the chants.

They were the same chants of praise and an invitation for Earl Dagon and Demon Vine to commune with us in the Order.

The nuns were most definitely sentries for the Earl.

"Alex..." I whispered. I needed to tell her—everything—and fast.

She waved me off and pointed.

From the back of the nave, on the left, another nun entered. Only, the nun who entered didn't really look much like a nun at all. More like a disheveled zombie; eyes wide, popping from their sockets. Her face was ashen white, with dark black circles surrounding her eyes. She raised her hands, and the chanting ceased.

She started speaking to the nuns...in the ancient language of the Witch Hunters.

I understood a few of the words.

None of them were good.

Alexandra looked at me, her eyes questioning. I

shrugged and motioned for us to leave. She ignored me and crouched behind the pew.

Dammit, that woman *looked* for trouble—and found it.

Or trouble found her.

Either way, I had to get her out of there.

"Alex, we need to leave. It's not safe here." I whispered, grabbing for her hand.

She snatched it back. "Blake, no. I need to find out what's going on."

We watched as the nuns formed a line in front of the head zombie nun. The zombie dipped wafers into a cup of what I suspected was wine.

They were taking communion.

My mind reeled with the weirdness of a bunch of demon-loving nuns partaking in a deeply rooted religious act, but I didn't want to stick around for the tea and cookies that followed.

I huffed. "Alex, I can tell you *exactly* what's going on here, but not *while* we're here. We need to go. Now."

She peered at me. "What do you know, Blake?"

"Not. Here." I said and moved from the hiding place, back into the vestibule. Once there, I straightened up, stretching. Difficult for a guy my size to stay crouched, and I had enough of that for one evening.

Alex joined me, tapping me on the shoulder and pointing to the door. We snuck out the way we came. We slunk out to the churchyard, then rushed into the gravesite beside it. I grabbed Alex's hand and pulled her through the graves, to the furthest, darkest corner.

I leaned against a large, crumbling headstone and took a deep breath. Alexandra, hands on her hips, stared me down.

"Alright, Blake. Spill."

CHAPTER

NINETEEN

ALEXANDRA

Blake leaned against the crumbling headstone, running his hands through his hair. The scent of his shampoo wafted through the dewy air, mixing with the scent of moss and old-growth trees. My stomach, already knotted with the stress of the evening, clenched further. I was disliking the scent of the shampoo I created and made a mental note to change the formulation.

"Blake," I said again. "Spill it. Now."

"I think I know why the nuns are after you."

I peered at him in the dim of the trees, his features masked by the shadows. "What do you mean, you know? What's going on, Blake?"

He took a deep breath. "The nuns are sentries for...Earl Dagon."

I stared at him. My pupils had to have been huge, trying to pull in whatever light they could. "Sentries? Of the Earl? But...why?" Somewhere in the distance, thunder rolled.

"Yeah. Apparently, Earl Dagon is, well, after you."

Every muscle in my body clenched. "After *me? But why?*"

Blake hesitated. I thrust my hands on my hips and looked him square in the face.

"Because you're...you're..."

"Oh, for the Goddess's sake, Blake—speak!"

"You're the last remaining ancestor of his bloodline..."

I shook my head. I knew I carried the Earl's evil blood in my veins, but the *last* remaining relative? This was news. "Okay, great, so I'm the last. When I'm gone, there won't be any more evil Dagon blood floating around the earth. That's good news, Blake. But it doesn't really explain why he's after me. If I'm dead, so is his lineage."

Blake pursed his lips and nodded. "Yes, true...but...you aren't just the last of his bloodline. There's more."

I rolled my eyes at him, not caring if he couldn't see the white of my eyes in the dark. "Oh, pray, enlighten me with your wisdom of all things, Dagon, Witch Hunter."

Blake shifted, jamming his hands into his jeans pockets. "You're the reincarnation of Evelyn of Cumbria. *His* Evelyn."

Blake's image swam before my eyes. My knees buckled, and I landed, hard, in front of a tall headstone. I swooned, leaning against the headstone for support. An image of the painting of Evelyn inside the castle exploded in my head. She didn't just *look* like me, she *was me*.

No. No, no, no, no, no.

I couldn't be.

"You're wrong. You have to be wrong." My voice was a mere raspy whisper.

Blake crouched in front of me, then sat on the wet ground, crossing his legs. "As far as I know, it's true. I'm sorry Alex."

I buried my head in my hands and sobbed. Blake shifted, moving closer, and slipped an arm around me. I leaned against him, grateful for his warmth and attempt to comfort me.

"I...I don't want to believe it, Blake. Cressy, my mentor, helped me see all of my past lives, and being Evelyn of Cumbria wasn't one of them. I can't live knowing that I'm responsible for..." I spread my hands and arms out, "...all of this..." my breath caught.

"All of this what, Alex?" Blake asked.

"The world, Blake. The death of hundreds of thousands of witches during Dagon's trials. I just *can't* be responsible. I'm a witch, for Goddess's sake!"

Blake pulled me tighter against him. "You aren't responsible, Alex. Earl Dagon created the Order of the Witch Hunters and the law."

"But, if Evelyn hadn't spurned him...had just stayed with him...none of it would have happened." I sobbed again.

"I'm sure you...I mean, Evelyn, had her reasons for leaving the Earl..."

"Sure. Because he's an evil, vile, demon—loving, witch —hating asshole." I grumbled.

Blake pulled his arm away and unzipped his jacket. The frosty night air hit my neck and shoulders and I shivered. He un-tucked his shirt, wiping my eyes, then my nose. I sniffed. "Thanks." But something niggled at me. "Blake, this doesn't really explain why the Earl sent demonic nuns to hunt me down, does it?"

Blake shook his head. "No. Well, maybe. I'm not sure."

"Do you know why, Blake?" I peered at him.

He hesitated, then nodded and looked me in the eye. "Apparently, he wants you to join him—and Madeline—on the throne, in...the afterlife."

I found my earring and tugged hard. *Of course, he did.*

Bastard.

As the story was told, he burned Evelyn on the pyre long before finding and marrying Madeline Bavant. He must have 'found' me again, and wanted a reunion, although I'm his last remaining blood relative.

Or maybe because of it.

Nothing made sense. My head throbbed, and my eyes were aching with tiredness and weeping. Blake slipped his arm around me again and I let him. I was too tired, angry, frustrated, and confused to fight.

I just wanted to go home, bury my head under the covers, and talk to Penny.

But, I couldn't talk to Penny. She was sequestered in the castle dungeon, about to be stripped of her powers, and burned at the pyre.

Could things get any worse?

"I need Penny, Blake." I peered up at him again, trying to read his expression. He just looked at me.

"I'm not sure I can help you with that, Alex."

"You know where she is." I knew he knew, but wanted him to admit it.

It took him several moments, but he nodded. "Yeah. I do."

"She's in the castle dungeon, protected by magic, awaiting death," I spoke flatly. I didn't care if he found out I was there. I didn't care about anything right now, except getting Penny back.

I wouldn't be responsible for one more death of a witch.

Not while I was still breathing.

"Are you asking me or telling me, Alex?"

"Both. Asking you to tell me what you know and telling you what I already do."

Blake removed his arm from my shoulder and clasped

his hands together in his lap. A cold, brisk wind chilled my shoulders. All at once, I wanted his arm back around me, but also wanted him as far away from me as possible.

He was still one of *them*.

I had to remember that.

"She's in the castle dungeon, yes. How do you know Alex? You were there, weren't you? At the Witch Hunter's meeting?"

I nodded my head.

"But...how? I didn't see you..." he rolled his head back and looked up at the cloudy night sky. "A glamor. You wore a glamor and joined the circle, didn't you?"

I nodded again.

"Alex! Do you have any idea how dangerous that was?"

"We were protected, Blake. Hence the glamor. It failed, though, when we went down to the dungeon to find Penny. The dungeon is protected *from* magic, *by* magic."

"*We*? Who's we, Alex? Did you take Teddy with you?"

I clamped my mouth shut.

Clearly, it was *way* too big.

"Never mind that. I need you to get her out, Blake. She shouldn't be in there."

Blake stood, shaking off the dirt. I joined him. "Why not, Alex? She's a witch. She deserves her fate."

"*What*?" I couldn't believe what I was hearing. A heavy, familiar, evil heat flushed through my body. "What happened to your taking responsibility for her being there in the first place, Blake? What happened to your promise to find her?"

He stood tall, crossing his arms. "I found her. She's in the dungeon. Nobody can get near her."

I shook my head. "You goddamned Witch Hunting *asshole*. You never planned to help us at all, did you?"

Blake held his ground. "I have a responsibility that you don't seem to understand, Alex. A responsibility to the Order, to my High Commander."

"The Sheriff? Who else is in the Order, Blake?"

Who did I have to kill?

Harm thee none, Alexandra.

But, this situation fell outside the witch's creed, didn't it?

Maybe a strike now, ask forgiveness later kind of thing?

Blake shook his head. "I can't divulge the member's identities any more than you'd divulge members of your underground society, Alex."

He had a point.

But, I could find out. I'd have to. Clearly, Blake would not help me get Penny back.

"Whatever, Blake. You're a real piece of work, you know that?" I growled, clenching my fists at my sides like a toddler throwing a tantrum. I turned away from Blake toward the headstone I had just used as a leaning post.

It was the largest and oldest headstone in the entire graveyard and towered over me. Bits of aging concrete had let go over the years, but the name of its occupant was still clearly etched in large, bold lettering:

Earl Dagon

1590–1690

Leader of men

Savior of all mankind

That did it.

Heat boiled through my veins. Thick, Dagon ancestral blood flooded to the surface of my skin.

And I let it.

My hands glowed like molten lava. I looked down at them, focusing — not on squelching the blaze, but forming it into two large balls of red—hot flame.

I heard Blake's gasp behind me. "Alex! What are you..."

I stopped listening. Blood roared through my ears, down my neck, and into my heart. All I could hear was the strong, rapid pulsing as the fireballs grew.

I glanced behind me at Blake. The glow from the fire-balls lit up the trees, the surrounding gravestones, and his face. His eyes were enormous, almost cartoonish.

Somewhere deep inside my being, a gust of hot breath rose to the surface.

I laughed.

Only, it wasn't my laugh. It was deeper, darker...

Evil.

I could feel the heat swarming through me. All at once, I felt incredibly powerful and incredibly dangerous. I looked at Dagon's gravestone, reading the inscription again.

I hated him with every fiber of my being.

I couldn't let his blood run through me, envelop me, call me to him.

With a scream and a push, I threw the fireballs toward his grave. They hit with a loud crack, like lightning cutting a swath through the sky. The headstone exploded. Bits of granite flew in every direction, hitting parts of my body and face, but I didn't even feel it. The fireballs did their damage, smashing it to pieces. The grass surrounding the gravestone lit with the heat of the flame, but quickly extinguished, too damp to encourage the flame.

I stood, arms at my side, breathing hard. The pressure in my veins slowly subsided as my breathing slowed.

I turned to look Blake in the eyes.

I could tell that he no longer recognized me.

TWENTY

BLAKE

"Alex, what the...?"

I didn't know whether to be terrified or turned on.

But I knew that I'd never been more attracted to Alexandra. Or more unsure of who Alexandra really was. "You blew up Dagon's headstone." I barely whispered, stepping back a bit and rubbing the bump forming on my forehead where a large piece of headstone connected.

Alexandra started walking past me. "Way to state the obvious, Blake."

I turned to follow her. "I could arrest you, you know. Should arrest you."

She stopped and turned. "Go ahead. I dare you." Her eyes pierced mine, and a stepped back. She reeked of anger. I would bet that she had absolutely no idea how truly powerful she was and wondered if she had ever unleashed that kind of fire before.

"What just happened, Alex?"

"I got mad."

"Mad at me?"

"Yes, Blake." She paused, wrapping herself in a hug. I wanted to wrap her up myself, but after her rather magnificent performance, and knowing how she reacted when she was pissed, I thought better of it. "But not just you. I'm mad Penny was kidnapped, mad at myself, my past life, my mentor, Dagon, this world... everything." Her words came out in a rush. I could see a glint of tears in her eyes spilling onto her cheeks.

"I've never seen you this mad before. I didn't know you could...could..."

"Explode?"

"Yeah. That."

"That was pure, raw, evil Dagon ancestral blood at its finest." She replied, smugly.

"Uhh. What?"

"You know I'm the last of the lineage, Blake. You told me so yourself. That—explosion—was coming directly from that bloodline."

"Oh." Although she was a few inches shorter than me, I suddenly felt small in her presence. Her determination and anger stirred something inside me I couldn't quite explain, but I desperately wanted to take her—here—in the cold graveyard shadows and...*mate*...

She stepped toward me, arms folded. "You've seen me explode before, Blake."

I quirked an eyebrow and rolled my eyes up, searching through the ol' memory banks. But other than that time a few weeks ago at the Sanatorium—nothing. That time was different. Less...fire and brimstone hot. "Don't think so...I'd remember something that intense."

She took another step toward me and shook her head. "Oh, you don't remember, because, right after I blew up our high school and injured half the football team and cheer-leading squad, Cressy threw a helluva good forgetting spell over the entire community. Not quite in time though. I was still punished as a troublemaker, but the spell he cast was enough that no one remembers *how* I did it."

I stood, staring. A crack of moonlight shone through heavy parting clouds and settled on the space between us. It was enough to light up her features. I could swear her usual green eyes were glowing crimson.

Memories flooded through me in a torrential rush. I recalled having my arm broken in high school and getting a bunch of cuts and scrapes, too. My teammates fared as bad or worse than I did. I remember the school looking a little like a bomb had gone off, but I wasn't sure *why*. I remembered getting hurt. I just couldn't remember *how*.

Now, I knew.

It was Alexandra and her ancestral Dagon blood.

The blood she revolted against so strongly, yet it was likely the most powerful thing about her. Right now, the most attractive thing, too.

The thing I loved the most.

That realization stopped me dead in my tracks. I knew I was attracted to Alex, but *love*? That was a word I'd rarely used in past relationships. A comfortable warmth spread through me just thinking about it.

Now, here she was, blowing up Dagon's gravestone, claiming her undying hatred for the legend and the world he created. How could she deny her ancestral powers? I mean, she was the last remaining heir to the Dagon throne —*how could she not appreciate that?*

"Alex, your powers...they're...magnificent." I moved

toward her, into the crack of moonlight. She peered at me, frowning.

"They aren't *magnificent*, Blake. They're terrifying and represent everything I hate about this world."

"But, your legacy—it's Dagon—you're the last remaining heir! You should embrace your power and accept your legacy! *You could rule!*"

She stepped away from me and bumped into a headstone. "*Rule*? Are you insane? *I'm a witch, Blake!* I do good deeds for Goddess' sake. *Not burn people on the pyre for who they are!*"

I stepped toward her, but she backed away, raising her hands in front of her. "Alex, think about it. We could be together—rule together—continue Dagon's bloodline... together..."

She stopped, eyes wide. "No, Blake. Not in a million years."

My heart sunk in my chest.

I tried to reason, "Earl Dagon wouldn't have any reason to want to kill you if you did. I—"

She raised a hand. I shut my mouth.

Small, sparkly energy tingled off of her hand like fairy dust and spread over the slight distance between us. Looking down and the golden swirls, I watched them attach to my heart center. I felt the fluid, warm heat of Alex's energy flow through me, comforting me. I looked up and lost myself in her beautiful green eyes, mesmerized. She was absolute perfection.

And I loved her.

She started chanting.

"Goddess good, Goddess great, make this man cooperate,

Ease his mind of troubled thought,
Make him forget me and the lot.
So mote it be."

TWENTY-ONE

ALEXANDRA

This was it. The end. I couldn't listen to Blake's praise of all things Dagon a minute longer. I had meant to throw a forgetting spell his way weeks ago, but after he had promised he wouldn't turn me in... well if I was being honest, I didn't *want* him to forget me.

Now, I did.

No way was I going to 'embrace' my Dagon blood. He was insane to even suggest it. Although, I could understand where it was coming from. All he knew was Dagon's truth. It was what he was raised on, along with the rest of the world.

And, ruling? With Blake at my side? Continuing the evil bloodline?

Forget it!

The tipping point had arrived. Clearly, there was no room for me in Blake's life, or for him in mine. But, if I rejected him again, I risked being captured and burned on the pyre—again.

How many times would I have to endure that bitter end?

I had to make him forget me and our brief history together. Then I could go about the business of figuring out how to release Penny—and run.

I pulled my witchy energy into the center of my being and raised my hand. Blake was sputtering some idiocy about sitting on Dagon's throne and having a dozen Dagon babies I didn't want to hear.

Couldn't.

It was now or never.

I stopped his jabbering and said the spell. It was a simple spell, really. For a single person, that is. When Cressy had cast the forgetting spell over the entire town... well...that was a different matter and manner.

And clearly, effective.

I watched Blake's eyes as I said the spell, swimming in the pools of deep brown, I hesitated for a fraction of a second, choking on the words.

This was it.

The end of Blake and Alex.

Not that there *was* a 'Blake and Alex.'

For certain, there would never be.

A searing heat flooded through my core. Not the evil Dagon heat, but something...sad. Remorseful. Tears sprang and dropped in large dots onto my cheeks and froze there in the chilly October air.

I was mourning the loss of something that could never be.

When the spell was complete. I kept my hand in place, holding my energetic grasp on his body, mentally preparing my brain and body to dart away. He would wake up and find himself alone in a graveyard, assuming he had slept-walked, or something equally weird.

I lowered my hand. Blake's eyes followed it, then looked up at me.

"You want me to forget you?"

I jumped and stepped back.

What the...?

It didn't work?

I opened my mouth to speak and closed it, then opened it again. "Blake?"

"Alex, what were you trying to do, make me forget you?"

I stared into his eyes and nodded my head.

"Why would you want to do that?" He sounded hurt.

"I—I — you...need to forget me, forget all about me."

"So, you cast a spell on me? Was that what that was?"

I nodded my head again.

He ran his hand through his hair, releasing my favorite not-so-favorite scent. "Well, it clearly didn't work."

"Clearly."

The question was, *why*?

I looked at my hands, turning them over and over. They'd been truly confused tonight—obvs. I closed my eyes and said a silent prayer to the Goddess to forgive me for unleashing the evil—crap. Not that the Goddess would strip me of my powers, but you could never be too careful.

"Alex, look—I'm sorry, ok? I got a little...carried away when I saw you unleash your...powers. I didn't mean to, um, insult you or whatever."

I took a deep breath and blew it out hard. "Fine, what-ever, Blake. I've gotta go." Turning on my heel, I walked toward home. I had some summoning to do.

Cressy and I needed to have a little chat.

Blake slid into step beside me.

He was turning into a wart you can't get rid of.

A warty toad.

A solid laugh flew from my mouth in a huff. Walking briskly, I tried my best to get as far from Blake as I could, but he was bigger, with a super-decent stride. I jogged, but he kept up with me, so I ran.

He ran.

I dodged around the road, in-between cars, shrubs, and trees.

He dodged.

I couldn't shake him.

I stopped.

He nearly took me out.

"Alex! What the hell? Why are you running from me?" The hurt I'd heard earlier returned. I flipped around, facing him, and raised my hands.

"Get any closer and I'll turn you into a toad." A snort escaped me.

He tipped his head and quirked a brow. "Really, Alex? The forgetting spell didn't work. What makes you think turning me into a toad would?"

Good point.

I looked at his face. His handsome image shifted and morphed into that of a toad, all warty and green. His long legs and arms appeared all green and slimy.

I put my hand to my mouth and laughed.

He put his hands on his hips and tilted his toady head the other way.

The toad in my exhausted, delirious imagination did the same.

I laughed some more. Insanity gripped me. It was as if

I'd licked a Sonora Desert Toad, its psychedelic goo tripping through my brain.

Gut-wrenching cackles and snorts exuded from me. Holding my stomach, I flopped onto the nearest yard—which, thankfully, was mine—and rolled, laughing, tears streaming down my face.

Blake stood over me, hands still firmly planted on his hips. The toady image was gone.

"Are you done?"

I nodded, wiping the tears and allowing my laughter to subside before speaking. Blake offered his hands, and I took them. He hoisted me up to stand. "I'm sorry, I'm just… feeling crazy right now. It's…everything, I guess." I took a deep breath and released it. Tiredness flooded my bones. My eyes felt heavy and gravelly. I needed sleep, but I also needed to talk to Cressy.

Blake stepped closer, moving his body a comfortable distance from mine. I could feel the warmth emanating from him and felt another wave of tiredness wash over me.

"Understandable, Alex. This was kind of…a big evening."

"Also, insulting, Blake."

"What do you mean?"

"You insulted me by asking me to embrace the part of me I've been trying to hide my entire life."

"Oh. That."

"Yeah, that. I'm not a Dagon, Blake. I'm a witch, and although I'm not sure *how* or *who* I inherited my abilities from, it's the side of me I choose to keep. Anything else is… unacceptable."

Blake jammed his hands into his jacket pockets and nodded.

"I understand. I'm sorry, Alex, I just…"

"I know, Blake. It's okay. I know you were raised to believe witches are evil, but we simply aren't. I don't expect you to like it or even agree." I thought about his insistence that his parents were killed by a witch but didn't want to edge that sword at the moment. "In fact, I expect you to arrest me and stick me in the dungeon with Penny."

Penny! In the complete insanity of the evening, I'd almost forgotten about my friend, sequestered in 'Chateau Dagon'. I had to get her out of there!

"I will not stick you in the dungeon with Penny, Alex. But I can't guarantee that someone else won't. The demonic nuns, for instance."

Right. The nuns from literal hell.

There was also that.

Also, what was up *with that?*

The urgency to communicate with Cressy sparked my energy. I had to find out the truth about my past life as Evelyn of Cumbria. An angry jitter slipped through me. I could kind of understand why Cressy kept that piece of info from me, but also, kinda didn't. As much as the information was devastating, it also drove me to be better and do better in *this life*.

I looked up at Blake. His eyelids dipped, closed, and opened again in a flutter. He was practically asleep standing up. Again, he didn't seem eager to arrest me. Doing so was against his Witch Hunter creed, to be sure.

Why, though?

Why didn't he arrest me, right from the start? It made little sense. He could have stripped me clean of my powers by now and watched me burn, but he hadn't. He believed what he was told as a teen—that his parents were killed by a witch—yet he still hung around...

I stepped closer as the thick cloud cover split between

us and the morning light kissed the sky. Looking up at him, deep into the pools of his dark brown, delicious eyes, I had my answer.

My breath caught.

Blake's eyes grew wide, and he stepped closer, closing the gap between us. I heard his sharp intake of breath before he grabbed my arms and pulled me into him.

I stared up at him, mouth parted, breathing his breath, feeling the bond between us grow in an instant. Blake lowered his head, holding my gaze. His hands slid into my hair, grasping the back of my head as his lips brushed against mine. He pulled back slightly and looked at me again. When I didn't resist, he kissed me, fully, deeply, hungrily.

And I kissed him back.

For a moment, there was no breathing between us, only exploration. Our tongues entwined as our hands did, in each other's hair, up and down each other's body. Then our breaths came in gasps between the urgency.

Finally, we stopped. Panting, breathing, eyes wide and glowing in the creeping sunlight, we watched each other in the fascination of a new beginning.

I gathered my strength and my breath.

"Do you...do you want to come inside...? I could make coffee..."

"Yes."

CHAPTER
TWENTY-TWO

BLAKE

The tiredness that I had been fighting fled with Alexandra's kiss.

The pulsing in my pants remained.

She kissed me. Or, rather, she kissed me *back*.

She didn't push me away this time. Despite how shitty the evening had gone, or maybe because of it, she let me get close.

And I loved her for it.

We walked into the house and settled into Alex's kitchen wordlessly. The morning sun was quickly rising along the Eastern horizon, torching her living room in a sunny glow, streaming through the doorways into the kitchen. I watched as Alex busily prepared her fancy fru-fru coffee. Daylight glinted off her raven-black hair, turning it to gold. I braced myself on the high island stool and watched her, mesmerized.

She finished preparing my coffee and slid it across the island. I took it gratefully and looked into the mug. A perfect hear-shaped, caramel-colored milky foam floated on the top. I grinned. "What, no genitalia this morning?"

She smiled. "Told you I've been working on it." She turned to prepare her own delicacy. When she was done, she slid onto the stool beside me. I arched my brows in surprise. Normally when I'd come for coffee, she kept the island between us.

Today was a special-as-heck day.

I raised my cup to hers and we 'cheered'. Sipping the foam off the top, I put the cup down, wanting to savor, not just the delicious coffee, but the equally delicious company.

"Blake?"

A trill of excitement buzzed through me as she said my name. "Alex?"

"There's someone that I'd like you to meet. I think you've earned it."

My eyebrows perked up. A noise came from the kitchen door and I stretched my head above Alex's seeing her black cat sauntering into the space.

"Hey there, kitty—kitty." I put one hand down and rubbed my fingers together, enticing the tootie boy to come my way.

He didn't.

Full stop. He sat and stared at me. I could swear he was frowning.

Alex giggled beside me. "Blackjack hate's the 'kitty, kitty' reference. It's beneath him."

"Oh, he does, does he? And how would you know?"

"I can hear him speak."

What the F?

"You can what?" My mouth caught up with my thoughts.

"Zoolingualism. I can hear animals speak." Alex said

130

matter-of-factly and took another pull of her coffee. Foam crested the top of her lip. It took all of my energy not to kiss it off. I had gotten *this* far. I was terrified of pushing it.

"Really." I grinned at her. "That a witchy thing?"

"Mmm, maybe." She smiled.

"Is this who you wanted me to meet? Because I kinda already met him before. Tootie cat. Often has a gaseous back-side..."

Alex threw a hand to her mouth, suppressing a giggle. Blackjack got up and continued his saunter past me, through the dining—room door, and into the living room, leaving a trail of rippling farts.

"He says he doesn't like you. Called you a behemoth caveman."

"He did, did he? Or maybe that was you...?"

Alex shook her head. "Nope. That was all Blackjack. He's a complete snob, but he's mine." She turned and looked into the living room fondly after him.

"So, if not the cat, then who?"

"Whom," she corrected.

"Sorry, 'whom'. Behemoth caveman here, remember?"

She tossed out a laugh. The sound was magic to my ears. After the argument we had and the fear of losing her ripping through me, it was the best sound I'd ever heard. In. My. Life.

"I think I'd like you to meet my mentor, Waldo Cress."

Whoa.

Who to the what?

"Is he like...your dad?" This was escalating quicker than I expected. I mean, *we had only just kissed*, and it felt like a long time coming.

Now she wants me to meet her mentor-dad guy?

Tiny nodules of gooseflesh fired through me. I was torn between excited anticipation and complete terror.

Alex smiled. "No, not my dad. I don't know who he was, remember?" I nodded. "Cressy is my mentor...from...the other side."

I quirked a brow. "Other side of what—town?"

That delightful laugh burst from her mouth again. "No, from the other side of life."

I placed an elbow on the island, leaned on my hand, and turned to look at her. "You mean, he's...dead?"

"Yes."

"I need sleep. Clearly, the coffee isn't kicking in and I've jumped the train to crazy town. Your mentor is dead? As in —a ghost?"

Alex tilted her head and frowned at me. "You put all your faith and trust in demons and evil, dead Earl, but you can't believe I commune with the ghost of my dead mentor?"

She had a point. Well, not quite. I put faith and trust in the Order, but for Alexandra, that faith and trust were quickly and quietly crumbling.

I was just a Witch Hunter, falling for a witch.

Take *that*, Notting Hill.

Not that I ever watched such goo. Or admitted to it, anyway.

"Okay, touché. I'll meet your mentor. Are you sure you want me to? I mean, it's kind of a big step...are we ready for this? It feels sudden."

Alex rolled her eyes at me and took my mug to the sink. "We aren't getting married, Blake. Just getting the information we need."

My heart did a little flip at the 'M' word, then settled.

"Okay, I'm game. What do we need to find out?"

"Well, mostly about the 'revelation' you told me about my past life. And maybe he could shed some light on the whole demonic nun situation."

I nodded. "Ahh. Good, yes. So, what do we do?"

"Just follow my lead, Blake."

I watched her walk into the living room, mindful to keep my eyes above ass level.

I followed.

TWENTY-THREE

ALEXANDRA

I was probably nuts for wanting to introduce Blake to Cressy, but I hoped, in doing so, I would solidify Blake as an ally, not an enemy.

Because he actually was still the enemy.

Until that kiss, anyway.

That 'knocked my pointy hat off, rock my loopy world,' kiss.

I had been tempted to invite Blake in for more than coffee, but my annoyingly sensible side kicked in. Better to take things with a dash of careful and a smidge of slow over what my body was yearning for.

Besides, in my delirium, I couldn't remember whether I'd worn my fancy panties.

Not a thong, that was a definite. I'd given up flossing my butt cheeks years ago.

Better to wait than take the chance.

I led Blake into the living room and pushed him onto the couch while I got the room ready to summon Cress.

Closing the heavy draperies and doors, slicing the early morning light from existence, I rolled up the antique carpet, pulled out the brass candleholders, black candles, salt, and small cauldron, and set up my circle.

Once the setup was complete, I held my hand out to Blake. He took it, got up from the couch, and stood beside me, inspecting the circle.

"I'm not a complete newbie regarding rituals, but your preparation is pretty outstanding."

"Not my first time. Shall we get started?"

Blake's eyes grew wide, but he grinned. "We? You mean you want *me* to help you summon a dead guy? Isn't that kinda third or fourth date stuff?"

I gave him a half smile. I took a moment to second—think my decision to include him, but was enjoying any chance to make him even the slightest bit uncomfortable, so I shook my head.

"Not today, Blake. However, I reserve the right to determine the activities for said third or fourth date, should said dates happen."

Did his cheeks just flush?

Score.

"So, what do I have to do?"

"Just focus on the cauldron smoke and repeat the incantation after me."

Blake nodded and looked down into the salt circle. Blackjack moved off the chaise and began pacing around the perimeter of the circle; his contribution to the task.

I started one round of the chant. Blake followed for the second round.

"Heaven to Earth, hear my plea, bring back he who watches over me.

Goddess and Gods of North, East, South, West, allow us to commune with our dear Cress."

The fire beneath the small cauldron snuffed. Tendrils of smoke reached upwards like cloudy fingers. I watched Blake's face as he stared, wide-eyed, at the smokey formation of my long—time mentor and friend.

Cressy, when fully formed, turned to me.

"*Alexandra*. What a pleasant surprise. To what do I owe this immense pleasure?" He slid his long, bony fingers of one hand into the pocket of his deep purple velvet smoking jacket and held a pipe with the other. His hair was slicked back in its usual fashion, and his pencil-thin mustache sat neatly on his upper lip.

"Hi, Cressy," I replied rather flatly. I was torn between excitement to see my friend and anger toward him for keeping my past life a secret. "We have things to discuss." I motioned to Blake. "This is Deputy Sheriff Blake Sheraton. He's also a Witch Hunter."

Cressy stood back, eyes wide. "Goodness gracious, Blake Sheraton. How you've grown. Tell me, am I under arrest? Or Alexandra, perhaps?"

Blake pulled himself to his full height, but as tall as he was, he was several inches shorter than Cress. "Hello, sir. Do you know me? And no, no one is under arrest."

"Well, thank goodness for small miracles." Cressy patted a hand to his heart and smiled, showing his yellowing, crooked teeth. "I remember you as the young man who gave my Alexandra a serious dose of abuse as a child."

Blake lowered his head. "Yes, I remember, sir, and I've apologized to Alexandra for that." He rubbed an imaginary spot on the floor with the toe of his boot.

"Did you, now? Well, that's mighty mature of you,

Sheriff Sheraton." Cressy looked from Blake to me. "What's troubling you, my dear? Are you still unable to locate Penny?"

The thought of Penny locked in the castle dungeon brought tears to my eyes. I let them fall. "Penny's been taken by the hunters and is locked up in Castle Dagon, Cressy. We know that for sure, now."

Cressy's brow furrowed. He tapped a long, yellowing nail on his chin. "I see. And Deputy Sheriff Sheraton is the one who took her?"

"No, sir," Blake piped up. "It was another Witch Hunter. Although...unfortunately, I was the one who alerted the hunters to Penny's existence."

"I see. Well, your presence here is my current puzzler to be worked out later. Alex, my dear, why have you summoned me? Do you want me to help you get Penny back? I'm not sure that's possible. The castle dungeon is under a protection spell-cast by Earl Dagon himself. It's held firm for centuries, I'm afraid."

"You know about the spell? You never told me!"

"The information didn't seem relevant. Teaching you to live the life of an underground witch was always my first priority. I hardly expected you to be caught. , " he glanced at Blake. "Or befriend your enemy..."

"Blake has apologized for his role in Penny's kidnapping. He's...on our side." I looked up at Blake. A solid rock of hope hung in my chest. Blake's smile lightened the load. "He also knows the truth about who I am, Cress. A truth you chose not to tell me." I frowned at my friend.

He lifted his eyebrows, then his head in acknowledgment. "Ah. Tell me, what information has the good Sheriff enlightened you with?"

"You know, Cress."

"Perhaps. But indulge me, won't you?"

"That I'm Evelyn of Cumbria. I was Earl Dagon's first love. The reason he created the world as we know it. The reason thousands of witches have burned on the pyre!" I shouted. Drops of spittle flew from my mouth and landed on the salt circle.

Cressy eyed me, took a deep breath, and nodded. "Yes, it's true."

"Why didn't you tell me?"

"For the same reason I came to be with you in the first place, Alexandra. To protect you while you learned what you needed to learn to cope—again—in this world."

I rested my face in my hands and cried. Blake slid a comforting arm around me. I tucked my face into his chest and wet his shirt with my tears.

"Alexandra," Cressy spoke, softly. "I know this is difficult to hear. Believe it or not, I wanted to protect your feelings. I hope you can understand that. I feel fully justified in my decision to do so."

I slowly nodded my head, wiping my tears and looking at Cressy through a wet blur. "I know, Cressy. Of course, you were always trying to protect me. I am grateful, just... confused."

"Is this why you summoned me? To see if it was true?"

I nodded. "Also, to see if you have any idea why a large pack of demonic nuns is after me."

Cressy's eyebrows shot up, and he stepped back. "Excuse me?"

Blake stepped closer to the circle. "Yes, sir. Alexandra's home and business have recently been vandalized. Then, just last evening, a group of demonic nuns—I counted eighteen in all—chased her home. They couldn't step on her property, though."

"Protection jars," I injected.

Blake raised a brow but continued. "She called me to help. We followed them to the church and witnessed another nun—assumably their leader—join them. They spoke in the ancient Witch Hunter language. The language created by Earl Dagon and the demon, Vine."

I turned to Blake, slapping his chest. "You could understand them? Wait, of course, you could. I recognized those chants. I heard the Witch Hunters chanting the same thing in the castle. Blake! Why didn't you tell me?"

"I couldn't understand all of it. Honestly, I just haven't had time to tell you. When you blew up Earl Dagon's headstone with your Dagon fireballs..."

It was Cressy's turn to inject. "*Alexandra!* You did what? What is going on here? Someone, please explain it to me!"

We explained.

After we'd brought Cressy up to snuff on the recent unfortunate events, he scolded me for allowing my Dagon blood to burst.

"That's exactly the kind of behavior that will get you thrown into the dungeon, missy."

Protesting, I nodded. "I know, I know, but I couldn't help it—didn't *want* to help it."

Cressy nodded. "You'd just received some rather harsh news."

"Yes. So. Do you know who the nuns are? Blake says they're sentries for Dagon and he wants to reunite with Evelyn of Cumbria, but nuns?"

"Better sit down, you two. This could take a while."

Blake and I sat side-by-side on the couch. The heat from his body fused with the heat in mine, making my heart flutter.

"Madeline Bavant was a nun in Louviers, France, in

1647. She had become possessed by a rather nasty demonic presence, and subsequently also possessed eighteen others. Earl Dagon, who had also succumbed to his dark inclinations, sought a replacement for his previous wife, Evelyn of Cumbria."

"You mean me," I interjected.

Cressy nodded solemnly. "Unfortunately, yes. He burned you alive on a pyre in Castle Dagon."

My stomach roiled. I put my elbows on my knees, held my head in my hands, and took a deep breath. "Go on."

"Upon hearing about Madeline's fall from grace, the Earl resolved to make her his new wife. They wed in Louviers and returned to Castle Point to reign."

There was more rambling about the Dagon's ancestors and the demise of hundreds of thousands of witches, but I'd stopped listening.

I was directly responsible for all of it.

If only I—as Evelyn of Cumbria—had stayed with the Earl —put up with his abusive ways—then none of this would have happened.

My heart dully thudded in my chest and my ears rang. Wave after wave of nausea ripped through me.

I sat and thought for a long while after Cressy finished his story. "So, if Dagon knew I existed, and he wants me to burn at the pyre again—or join him and Madeline on his throne—whatever—why didn't he insist on having his sentries kill me as a child?"

Cressy ran a finger along his thin mustache. "It's quite possible that he didn't know you had returned to the land of the living. Not until recently, anyway. I'm afraid I really cannot say, Alexandra."

Blake chimed in. "Maybe it has more to do with your

age. Cressy, how old was Evelyn of Cumbria when Dagon burned her on the pyre?"

Cressy's brow creased. "She was thirty-eight if I recall."

Another wave of nausea hit me. I could feel the blood drain from my face and pool at my feet.

"Alexandra, what is it? What's wrong?" Blake asked,

"I turn thirt-eight on Samhain," I whispered.

TWENTY-FOUR

BLAKE

This couldn't be happening.

Black dots swam before my eyes. I leaned back on the couch and breathed deeply, wiping my eyes. The dots were still there. I grabbed for Alex's hand, but she pushed up off the couch and ran to the bathroom, barely closing the door before she retched. My stomach wanted to follow her, but my eyes couldn't see straight. I closed them and breathed some more.

When I opened them, Cressy was still hovering inside the circle, assessing me with his ghostly eyes. I pressed my lips into a thin line and nodded toward him.

A slight bow of reverence.

I was acknowledging a ghost, for God's sake.

Could my life get any weirder?

"What is your part in all of this, Blake? You're a Witch Hunter. Surely you've had your sights set on my girl. Has Earl Dagon and his army of demonic nuns foiled your plan to capture and kill my Alexandra?" Cressy's tone was understandably upset.

"No, sir. Well, maybe when I first found out Alex was a witch, it was. But, not now."

"And why not? You've been anything but kind to Alex when you were younger. Why start now?"

"I know, sir. And I believe Alexandra has forgiven me for our...past. I've seen the good she can do, sir, and I...I...have developed...." I couldn't continue. The man before me wasn't just Alex's ghostly mentor. I imagined he was the father she never had. Speaking to him put my nerves on edge.

"You have feelings for her? Romantic feelings?" Cressy asked, and I slowly nodded. "I see. You were raised in the lineage of the Witch Hunters, Blake. Forgive me if I find it difficult to believe that you could change your opinion about the witch race now."

"I understand that it's confusing, sir, based on my history with witches. My own parents were killed by one, you see."

A great roar of laughter came from Cressy, startling me. I frowned. "It's true, sir. At least, that's what I've been told. I have no reason to believe otherwise."

Cressy wiped a ghostly tear from his eye as his cackling subsided. "I'll bet my eternal life it was *not* a witch, Deputy Sheriff." Cressy smoothed his mustache. "Or, if it were, she or he had their back against a wall and acted out of sheer terror."

I opened my mouth to protest when Alex walked in.

"What did I miss?"

"Nothing." Cressy and I said together. Alex eyed us both and sat down.

"Blake and I were just getting better acquainted, dear. Feeling better?"

"Somewhat. Something occurred to me when I was jettisoning my coffee."

"What was that, dear?"

"Well, I have to assume that the nuns were the ones who vandalized my business..." Cressy raised a brow. "...spray painting 'witch' on the building in red," Alex explained. Cressy nodded. "But there were also symbols. Much like the ones we found in Mitch's cell and..." Alex stopped.

"And...?" I asked.

Alex looked at me, but there was something dark and hollow in her eyes. "Nothing. Just that, the symbols looked so much like that, but...different."

I nodded. "The language Earl Dagon and the Demon Vine created and taught the Witch Hunters."

Cressy and Alex looked at me. "You said that before. I didn't know you knew it, Blake. Why didn't you tell me earlier? When we were at the sanatorium with Mitch Myles weeks ago?"

I folded my hands in my lap. "Because I wasn't sure then...about...you. I didn't know how much I could tell you."

Alex nodded, pulling out her phone and scrolling through her recent photos. She showed Cressy the picture she had texted me. I hadn't replied to that text. I didn't really know what to say.

"So, what does it say?" She asked, handing me the phone.

I read the symbols. "It just says 'witch' and also..." I paused, "that your fate is sealed..."

"That's it?"

"Yeah. That's it."

Alex narrowed her eyes at me. "You're sure?"

I nodded. "Sorry, Alex."

She sat, staring at the photo, thinking. "What did the symbols say on Mitch Myles's cell walls, Blake?"

I paused. Longer this time.

I couldn't tell her that the symbols Mitch drew on his cell walls were the key to the complete destruction of the Order of Witch Hunters.

Not yet, anyway.

I felt a searing heat run a jagged spear through my chest, down to my stomach. It was like two halves of me were ripping apart. One half, a born-and0-bred Witch Hunter, tied to the Order. The other, a confused, do-gooder falling for a beautiful, kind witch, leaning hard to her favor.

If the High Commander ever found out that I'd interpreted the demise of the Order, he'd have my head.

If I didn't tell Alex the truth, I'd risk losing her, either by her merely being pissed at me, or to a batch of past-white demonic nuns.

My head split as much as my heart had. I couldn't decide.

"I'm not exactly sure, Alex."

She peered at me. "You're sure?"

I nodded. She opened her mouth, but, thankfully, Cressy stepped in.

"Children, as much as I'd like to have the interpretations myself, I think we should focus on the issue at hand, agreed?"

We agreed.

"Very good. Alex, the first order of business, is expelling the demon's curse from the nuns. I think you should use what you have at your disposal."

"Meaning...? A spell?"

"A potion."

Alex nodded. "Sure, but how would I get them to take it?"

A light flashed above my head. "Communion! Alex, we watched them take communion last night. You could spike their communal wine!"

Alex stood up and started pacing. "That could work! I could get Teddy to create a potion for expelling the demonic presence. We'd have to figure out how to get it into their wine, but once we do..."

"That could work, yes. Except I would think it's likely they have demonic guards," I added.

Alex pulled at her earring. "Something just occurred to me, Blake. We haven't seen Father Donovan. I wonder where he is? Did the demon possess him too?"

"No clue, but I'm sure we could find out. Any ideas on how to get into the church undetected?" I asked the question but was pretty sure I already knew the answer.

"A cloaking spell." Alex and Cressy answered in unison.

I was pretty new to the witch game, but I kinda figured; magic.

"Okay, I'm down for a little cloaking. We should do this tonight, Alex. Once we get rid of the demonic nuns, we can focus on getting Penny back."

Alex smiled.

My heart melted.

CHAPTER
TWENTY-FIVE

ALEXANDRA

Cressy looked from me to Blake and back to me. "It seems you have everything in hand, Alexandra. If you require my assistance further, you know how to find me..."

I smiled at my mentor. "Thank's Cress. I appreciate... everything."

"So, I'm forgiven, then? For keeping your past life a secret?"

"You are. Of course you are." Warm tingles spread through my body. Honestly, I'd forgive him for anything. In life, and in death, he was my best friend.

Cressy waved as he vanished, leaving me, Blake, and Blackjack alone in the room. I glanced at Blake. He was staring at Blackjack, currently grooming his fur. A toot escaped his back end. Blake chuckled and shook his head.

Blake knew about the symbols and didn't tell me.

I wasn't sure how I felt about that. But then, why would he admit it? He was a member of the Order, sworn to rid the world of all things witchy. Why would he put his trust in me and give away their secrets? Of course, he'd kept it to himself. Until now, anyway.

I chided myself for almost opening my mouth about my mother. Although I hadn't straight up told Blake about my mothers 'condition' and her residence in Lexington Psychiatric Hospital, I let him assume my mother was dead.

I didn't bother to correct him.

I didn't want to go there, not now, not yet.

Besides, there may be no point. If we can't defeat the nuns and their purpose, I'd be keeping Penny company on the pyre.

I shuddered.

"You okay, Alex? You're pretty quiet."

"Just...thinking." The weight of sleep settled on my bones. "And I'm exhausted. I know we need to make a plan for a potion, but I can't keep my eyes open. I need a nap, Blake."

He nodded. "Of course. I'm pretty tired too. I need to check in at the office, though. Why don't we both nap and I'll come get you later?"

I nodded in agreement, slightly torn by wishing he suggested napping together and thankful he didn't.

Although the kiss was amazing, there may not be a point in throwing kindling on that spark.

Everything depended on the potion.

"Sounds good. I'll call Teddy and have her start the potion-making in the meantime. Hopefully, she can have it ready by tonight."

Blake got off the couch, stretched, and walked to the door. Pulling on his coat, he turned to me. I raised my head, anticipating the brush of his lips against mine, but he pulled the door open instead.

"See you soon, Alex."

I nodded and closed the door, squelching the tiny flame that had ignited in my core.

"Focus on the Hocus-Pocus, woman." Blackjack's thoughts interrupted my burgeoning fantasy.

"Right. You're right. Potion first, hot Sheriff later. Got it."

I reached for the phone and dialed Teddy's number. She answered on the first ring.

"What's up, Witchy Wonder Woman?"

"Hey, Teddy. A couple of things. Have you checked in with Cathy today, by chance?"

"Indeedie I did! She's holding up. I think she's grateful for the hounds' company right now. When I called her, she was taking them out for their early morning walkies. I instructed her to stay away from the castle, though. The last thing we need is for her to attempt to jailbreak her wifey and end up..."

She paused, but I nodded, my eyes closing where I stood.

"Agreed. Good thinking."

"Was there something else? You said a couple of things..."

"Yes!" My eyes snapped open. "Super important, actually. I need you to create a potion!"

"Ooooo—let me guess—a love potion? To use on the hot Sheriff with the super tight ass?" She giggled.

I wanted to join in on the giggle, but exhaustion squelched it. "No, Teddy. Although I reserve the right to ask for that later. This is way more important. Let me explain..."

I filled Teddy in on the past few hours, yawning between sentences.

"Holy broomsticks! Demonic nuns and the rise of Earl

Dagon? Sounds like the title of a super creepy movie. What did you have in mind? For a potion, I mean?"

"Well, I was hoping to lean on your expertise as a Master Herbalist, but I have a couple of ideas."

"I'm all ears and pencils over here—shoot."

"Well, typical for an exorcism, we'd use three parts Rosemary, one part Bay Leaf, and one pinch of Cayenne per person, but, since we have to spike an entire bottle of wine, and assuming the demonic nuns still have a sense of taste, the Cayenne might be a bit much."

I could hear Teddy's pencil scribbling notes on her paper. "Mm-hmm, yes, yes, true, true. I could use Yarrow and Rue instead. That would give a better flavor. Be less conspicuous, but pack more of a punch."

"That sounds divine, Teddy. Thank you. Think you could have it ready for tonight?"

"That's a heck to the yes, boss witch! I'll get on it right —stat now."

"Thanks, Teddy. I'm gonna hit the hay for a couple of hours, then I'll meet you at the shop." Her exuberance was appreciated, but right now, the bed was calling.

Also, a steamy, hot shower.

And a steamy hot fantasy about a steamy hot sheriff.

"Just the shower and bed, if you please, missy. I don't need to hear your lurid, disgusting thoughts on fornication."

Blackjack again.

Out to ruin my fun, as per his usual.

"Yes, boss. Wake me up when the sun hits 'fade'."

CHAPTER
TWENTY-SIX

BLAKE

I left Alexandra's and headed to the sheriff's department, my mind and body reeling. I didn't want to leave Alex to nap alone, but didn't want to push it either. I put the thoughts about spooning Alex back on the shelf to save that for later.

Besides, there was too much to do, starting with figuring out a way to get Penny out of the dungeon cell she was in.

I parked, turned off the car, and sat, shaking my head. Was I nuts for wanting to save Alex's friend? She was a witch and her powers rightfully belonged to the hunter who took her. At least, that's the way it's always been. 'Witches were evil and had to be dealt with'. It was the rhetoric I'd heard my entire life, starting with my father, who was High Commander at one point during his life.

But his life was taken by a witch. Could I really ignore that? Cressy and Alexandra most definitely didn't agree with my story, but they were both witches, so why would they?

Evil witches.

Except they weren't, were they? Alexandra was a good person, who helped many people and stirred something in me I'd never felt before. If I left Penny to burn on the pyre, I'd lose Alex for sure.

It was all about Alex.

The last remaining bloodline of the Dagon Kingdom. And she refused it.

What she wanted was her friend. And I seemed to be the only person who had a chance of giving that to her, but I'd go against every Witch Hunter law to do so. My father would be flipping in his grave if he knew I'd fallen for a witch.

Not to mention, I could be killed for the betrayal. So, there was also that.

Was Alex really worth it?

I walked into the department. I wanted to talk to Gordon, but he was at the Mayor's office for a meeting. Likely hunter business, not official duty.

Samhain, or Hallows Eve—depending on if you were a witch or a hunter—approached, which meant the demise of witch Penny and—if the wacko demonic nuns had their way—Alex, too. My stomach lurched. Thoughts of Alex burning on the pyre filled my head. She was such an amazing person. How could I let her burn?

No. It can't happen.

It started with getting Penny out of her cell. But how? I glanced around the bullpen. Most of the officers were busy on the phone or playing solitaire on their computers. Perfect opportunity to slide into Gordon's office and search for the skeleton key.

I turned the knob and stepped inside. Gordon's office was tidy. His OCD wouldn't allow anything less. I peered through the blinds into the bullpen. No one noticed, so I turned the blinds closed. Starting at Gordon's desk, I pulled open the top middle drawer. His pens, pencils, ruler, and office supplies were neatly organized in their assigned slots in a plastic organizer.

I closed the drawer and tried the next. More supplies and envelopes. I tried the next and the net. Files neatly labeled took up space in the bottom larger drawers. I rifled through the folders, but—no key.

I heard Larry address Gordon as he walked into the station. The Mayor Jeffrey Deibert was with him. Quickly closing the last drawer, I slid to the door, opening it a crack as sweat tickled my brow. Gordon stopped at Deputy Daniels's desk to answer a question. I slipped from his office and casually walked into mine.

I quickly sat at my desk just as Gordon and Jeff stepped into my office.

"Morning, Blake."

"Morning sir. Mayor." I stood and nodded toward them both.

The Mayor extended a hand, and we shook. "Howdy there, Blake."

"What can I do for you fellas?" I invited them to take a seat in the chairs opposite my desk. I rested one butt cheek on the edge of my desk and clasped my hands in front of me to stop my quivering fingers. The nervousness shot down to my feet instead, and they tapped madly. Gordon glanced at them, forcing me to stop.

Act normal, Sheraton. Not like you just came from a witch's house after conjuring the ghost of her dead mentor.

"We've been discussing the sacred hunter ritual, organizing preparations for stripping the little red-headed witch of her evil talents." Jeffrey drawled.

I cringed inwardly. "Oh, is that so?" I never found out who actually captured Penny at the meeting, and whoever it was didn't reveal himself. "Who was the—ahem—lucky hunter, if you don't mind my asking?"

Gordon pointed a thumb at Jeff. "This guy right here!"

My eyebrows shot up, and I slowly nodded my head. "Ahh. I see. Well, congratulations Mayor."

Jeffrey guffawed. "Now, Blake, I know you had your sights set on the evil little thing, but we all got a little tired of waiting for you to make the move, so...first come first serve, as they say."

"Sure. I understand. First, come and all that...well, congrats again."

Jeffrey barely heard me. "Yessiree. She was quite the catch if I say so myself. Fought like a little banshee, kicking and screaming. Yowee! Almost a shame to burn her, with that delicious big booty of hers..."

I coughed and peered at him.

"Now, now, Sheraton. You had your chance." Gordon wagged a finger at me.

I slowly nodded, pursing my lips. "Yes, well. I guess you win." Every muscle in my jaw, fist, and temples flexed. I swallowed the bile slowly creeping up the back of my throat. "When is the ritual?"

"Tomorrow on Hallow's Eve. Her powers will be stripped just before setting her ablaze."

My head swirled. I clutched the edge of the desk hard as I clenched my jaw harder, the muscles in my face guitar-string tight and ready to break.

Jeffrey chimed in, "Should be a real red-hot deal. The flames will burn as hot-orange as her hair. Yeehaw!"

I stood up and went to the door, grasping the handle. I needed air, fast. "That's impressive gentlemen, thanks for stopping by. Sorry, I've got to head out. Forgot I have...an attempted burglary to report." I opened the door and stalked through the bullpen. Glancing back, I saw Gordon and Jeffrey gaping after me.

Outside, I breathed the frosty October air, willing the storm in my stomach to settle. Exhaustion crept into my bones, so I jumped into my squad car and headed home to take a nap.

But who was I kidding? There'd be no napping today. There was too much to do. I needed to figure out a way to break Penny out of the jail she was in. I drove around aimlessly, thinking.

I knew Gordon had the key to Penny's cell. I couldn't find it hiding in his desk, which likely meant it was on him, and if I was in his position, I'd keep it on me, too. It wasn't like I could frisk him and take it, so exactly how I was going to break Penny out was a little beyond me. I'd have to figure out another way.

I'd have to wait until the ritual stripping of her powers to free her.

But then what? We'd both be hunted and killed. I liked Penny, and I liked—okay, *loved*—Alex, but I wasn't exactly prepared to leave my life behind for the sake of Alex's friend.

Or die.

There had to be another way.

My vision blurred, and my head bobbed. I pulled into a parking spot near the ocean and turned off the engine. Looking out across the rocky beach over the choppy water from my warm car, my eyes closed. Snapping them open, I tried to focus on the shore ahead of me, but my tired vision hazed. I saw a blur in the familiar shape of a human way down the shoreline, a fuzzy, rather eerie form far out in front of me.

It kinda looked like my dad.

Heat pricked my heart as I sat up a little straighter, rubbed my eyes, and shook my head, looking toward the same spot I saw the blurry shape just a moment ago.

Nothing.

My mind was officially having a meltdown from lack of sleep. I let out a huff of air and leaned back against the seat, narrowing my eyes and scanning the rocky shores. Tiredness crept in, flooding my brain like a warm blanket.

I thought about turning the car on and heading home for a nap, but that just seemed like too much work. I checked the time. Still early. Alex would still be asleep for a while anyhow, before heading to her shop to meet up with Teddy, so I may as well catch a few. I reached to the left of my seat and pulled the lever to lean all the way back.

A thud and squawk woke me, my heart racing. A large Pelican had used the hood of my squad car as a parking lot and cleaned itself while pooping gross gray-green goo onto my car. I honked and flicked the windshield wipers on. The bird gave me a look and flew off into the darkening sky.

Dammit. I slept way too long.

I turned the ignition and revved the engine into action. I shot a quick text to Alexandra asking if she was up and at the shop, but no reply. I threw the car into reverse, pulled out of the parking lot, hesitated for a second, then headed toward Alex's shop, certain she'd be there by now.

Brushing my fingers through my hair and popping a piece of gum into my mouth, I burned through town. As I approached Alex's store, I could see her car out front. A slight smile tugged at my lips and a tiny fire blazed in my belly. I actually couldn't wait to see her again.

The stores were all closed, and the street was practically empty, so I pulled into a parking spot beside her car and shut the engine. Jumping out, I rushed to the front door and found it unlocked. That seemed a little risky, so I closed it and locked it behind me.

"Alex? Teddy? Where you at?"

"Back here!" Teddy called out. I strode to the back of the shop, to the door leading into the back room, and pulled. Immediately, the sharp scent of herbs tickled my nostrils, and I wanted to sneeze. Holding my fingers to my nose, I took a moment to glance around. I'd been buying my shampoo there for years, in the shop's front where everything was painted stark white with matching stark white labels on the jars and bottles, the only other decoration being a lot of green plants. I did not know what was in the back room. Shelf after shelf, full of small and large jars of... *stuff*...wrapped around the dusty, dark room.

"Teddy? Alex?" I called again, walking further into the room. To my left, Teddy appeared, wearing an apron and rubber gloves, her colorful hair piled askew on top of her head.

"Hey, Blake! Great, you're here." Teddy craned her head to look behind me. "Did you bring Alex?"

I froze. "She isn't in here?"

"Nope, haven't seen her. She should have been here about an hour ago. I had everything under control, so I didn't want to call and bug her, but it's getting late!"

"Her car's out front." My heart started beating faster.

"Oh, really? Alex? You here?" Teddy called out, pushing the door open and walking into the front of the store. I followed her.

Glancing around, Teddy went to the front door.

"I locked it. Maybe she stepped in, then out again?"

"Maybe...hang on, I'll check the bathroom." Teddy stepped to the side of the shop and pushed the bathroom door open. "Nope."

"She must be outside." My hand shook slightly as I unlocked the door, grabbed the door handle, and pulled. A gush of cool air hit my face. If I wasn't quite awake when I arrived, I definitely was now. Teddy followed me outside. She walked one way down the sidewalk, I walked the other.

"Alex?" I called out. Teddy did the same behind me.

No answer.

I peered inside a couple of store windows and tried a couple of doors, but everything was locked up and dark. I walked back toward her car and tried the driver's door. It was unlocked. Opening it, I stooped down and glanced inside. Alex's handbag was in the back seat. My nerves jacked as I reached a shaky hand into the back seat to retrieve it.

Teddy joined me. "That's Alex's bag. Is anything missing?" I passed the bag to her. It felt like lava between my fingers. I leaned against the car while Teddy rifled through it. "Her wallet is here, and her phone..." she checked the phone. I could see my most recent text message there, unanswered.

I glanced down at my shoes. Something red caught my eye. "Teddy, step back for a sec." She did. I squatted beside the red mark, putting my finger on it and pulling back a digit with red...blood.

"Oh my Goddess, Blake, is that..."

"Yeah. Blood." I croaked out around an ominous lump in my throat.

"No, no, no." Teddy cried.

I stood up, looking around once more, but what was I looking for?

Alex was gone.

CHAPTER
TWENTY-SEVEN

ALEXANDRA

"Soon, my love. We will be together soon." Earl Dagon was lying beside me, cradling my head and stroking my hair. I felt an intense heat on my head from his hands, and it shot down my body. My head throbbed in a timed rhythm with my groin. I felt the urge to pull toward, touch, and grind against him. No! I pulled away, but my head ached. I squeezed my eyes shut, willing the pain—and the Earl—to vanish. I opened my eyes and saw the Earl's mouth descending on me...

I screamed. 'No. Never. You can't have me.' I pushed him away, but he kept coming, calling my name. The more he called, the harder I pushed until his voice shifted, and became more... feminine. I stopped pushing and listened.

I woke up with a sharp intake of breath and immediately tried to sit up. Another dream. A stabbing pain shot through my head. I grasped it and laid back down, holding my head in my hands. I felt a wet heat and pulled my hands away, peering at them with one eye open.

Blood.

Where was I? Home? I lay there, trying to open both eyes. Everything was so dark and my bed...it was cold, hard as...stone? The air around me felt cool, damp, and musty. I knew I wasn't the best housekeeper, but my place didn't smell like this.

Not my home. Not my bed.

Forcing my eyes open, I could see I was lying on my side, on a stone floor...but, where? I looked into the darkness. A pale, round, blurry object sat across from me. Was that...?

"Penny?"

Penny's face slowly came into view in the distance as my tear-filled eyes cleared. It was Pen! Was she out of her cell? Had she been released?

"Alex, wake up! You were talking, screaming, staring straight ahead. Who were you talking to?"

The back of my head throbbed, and I rubbed a hand to the area, wincing when I felt a large goose egg. "Penny, what? Where...? Am I...?" The metallic taste of blood and a tongue that felt too big for my mouth made it difficult to speak.

"You're in the castle dungeon, Alex! They brought you in a few hours ago. They must have knocked you out cold. I've been yelling at you, but nothing."

I squeezed my eyes shut and shook my head, trying to clear whatever cobwebs were wrapped around my brain, but it hurt too much. I opened my eyes and glanced around the dim room.

Holy Goddess, I was in a cell.

The bastards got me.

Penny! I scrambled to my knees and shuffled toward the

cell bars. Grasping the bars for support, I pushed my face against them and looked, wide-eyed, across the dungeon room at Penny, her face pressed against the bars in the same way.

"Penny," I breathed. "Oh, thank Goddess."

"I wouldn't be too thankful yet, witchy sister. If you hadn't yet noticed, were in the same pickle pile." Penny said, tapping the cell bars.

Right. "Oh, shit."

"Yep. Super shit-static. Agreed."

My thoughts flew to Blake. "Did you see who brought me in?"

"Yeah. It was a whacked-out group of gnarly-looking dudes in nun costumes and a couple of Witch Hunters. We will, of course, circle back to the gnarly nuns later, once your head clears."

A strange mixture of relief and fear flooded through me. Blake hadn't turned me in. That was something. But...*those bitches!* The demonic nuns grabbed me when I was away from the safety of my property.

The back of my head throbbed. I ran my hand over it.

"They must have whacked you hard to knock you out for so long."

I nodded. "Yeah." I rubbed my temples, trying to remember what happened. It took a while for the web to clear, then it came to me. "Blackjack woke me from my nap. We got in my car and headed to the shop to see Teddy's progress with the potion. Then everything went black. That's when they must have taken me."

"What potion?" Penny asked.

"Teddy was working on a potion to expel the demonic presence from the nuns."

"Demonic nuns? That would explain why it looked like they got into a fight with a car full of clowns over a tube of liquid eyeliner and white pancake makeup. Still, you're gonna have to read me the full novel, Alex. The cliff note version won't do. Besides, we have time." Penny tapped the bars again.

I told Penny everything, ending with Dagon's plan to reunite with me on my birthday.

"Samhain?"

"Yeah. Penny, Samhain. It's…" I blinked rapidly. I had no clue what day it was.

"Tomorrow, Alex. It all goes down tomorrow…"

I slumped onto the floor, leaning against the bars for support. A revolting feeling jolted through my belly and I heaved. Blood and gunk came up and spattered red goo on the floor.

"You okay over there?" Penny, the caring, kind nurse, asked.

"For someone who was just knocked on the head, kidnapped, and just threw up the entire contents of my stomach…just swell."

"Alright then. As long as you're swell."

A mewing drew my attention toward the dark corners of the cell.

"Blackjack?" I called.

"Yes, woman. Who were you expecting, the big lug of a Sheriff? Good luck with that."

"Blackjack! Where are you?" I grabbed the cell bar for support and tried to stand, but the blood in my head rushed to my toes and another wave of nausea stopped me. I flopped down again. Blackjack appeared in the high cell window and slipped through the bars, jumping down and skittering over to me. I stroked his beautiful, cool fur as he pushed his head against my hand, whipping his tail in the air. "How'd you know I was here?"

"When the bizarre nuns attacked you, I jumped out of the car, ran past them, and into the bushes. Then I followed you here. I've been waiting for you to wake up." He pushed his body into mine. His warmth comforted me.

"Blackjack? How?" Penny asked from across the room.

"He was in the car when I was attacked. He escaped, then followed me here."

"That's great, Alex. Did he bring the skeleton key, perhaps?"

Bless Penny and her humor. A small chuckle escaped me. "I don't think so, but he can still get us some help."

"Oh sure, how do you expect me to do that? Call the Deputy Sheriff? The burly idiot can hardly remember my name, let alone understand what I'm saying. I wouldn't say he's one poop away from a full litter box, but he's close. Probably the overcompensation of testosterone."

"Blackjack, enough!" I silenced the mangy brat thought for thought.

Penny chimed in. "How do you figure he can help, Alex? Use his little kitty paws and punch Blake's number into a phone?"

Blackjack looked up at me in agreement. *"I can do a lot of things, woman, but calling the cavalry isn't one of them."*

"Please try, Blackjack. Try to let Blake and Teddy know where I am. Can you do that?"

"Fine. But don't hold your breath. Actually, DO hold your breath. This place smells like week-old kitty litter." Blackjack shook his head, tooted, and sneezed.

I wanted to laugh, but my head hurt, so I ruffled his head and stroked his fur.

"Do your best, Mister, please?"

" I always do."

"Well, we don't have time to debate that now. Just go."

Blackjack sped back to the wall, scrambled up the stone wall to the cell window, back through the bars, and was gone.

CHAPTER

TWENTY-EIGHT

BLAKE

"Blake, what are we going to do?" Teddy whispered through a gulp and sniffle. I stopped looking up and down the street and focused on her instead. Her heavy eye makeup cast eerie rivers of black and purple down her cheeks. I untucked my shirt and brought a corner up to her face, not caring if the goop would permanently stain my shirt. Teddy let me wipe the tears and stains away, then grasped a fresh side of my shirt and blew her nose.

Okay, so the shirt was toast.

I peeled off my heavy fall jacket, slipped off the shirt, and handed the whole thing to her. She looked at me with black and red-rimmed eyes. I pushed it toward her. "Go ahead, do your worst." She smiled a wobbly one and took it, using the whole thing as a Kleenex. Shivering, I dug around in the back seat of my car and found a somewhat clean replacement. This one, I tucked in, slipped my coat back on, and zippered it fully, so she wouldn't get any ideas when a fresh snot rag was required.

"I think we stick to the plan, Teddy. If the nuns got her, we fix that problem first. Maybe in doing so, we'll find out where they took Alexandra."

"But maybe it'll be too late." Teddy blew her nose again and attempted to hand me the shirt. I put up my hands.

"Keep it. You might need it later. The ceremonial sacrifice isn't made until midnight, so we have some time. Let's get to work."

Teddy led me back into the shop and through the connecting door. Rounding a corner, she motioned toward a door to another room. The potion room, by the looks of it. A large, diminishing flame sat below an iron cauldron hanging from a rod going from one side of an enormous fireplace to the other. If I bent my body in half, I could've fit inside the length and depth of the fireplace easily.

The room smelled funky. I plugged my nose and wafted my free hand through the air. "What's that smell?"

"It's the potion." She pointed to the cauldron. The fire had almost burned out, the contents of the cauldron steamed, but not boiling and toiling, as one would expect when one sees the contents of an actual witch's cauldron.

Still holding my nose, I asked, "What's in it? Rubber boots?"

Teddy gave me a look. "No, silly willy. It's mostly herbs to combat curses and demonic possession."

I nodded my head. "I see, so, like, exorcism?" Teddy nodded. "And what herbs would those be, if I might ask?"

"I'll tell you while we bottle some of this stuff up. We have to hurry. We don't have oodles of time, Blake."

"Shit, right, let's go."

Teddy grabbed a couple of fresh amber glass bottles with screwtops. I held the bottles over the cauldron while

Teddy used a turkey baster to suck up and transfer the smelly mixture.

"It's a combination of Rosemary, Bay leaf, garlic, then Yarrow and Rue to top it off."

"You think that will work? They won't notice if the flavor of the wine is weird?"

Teddy looked at me like I was the dumbest person in the world. "We have to hope that they don't notice. I mean, they're *possessed*, so I'm betting they won't know the difference."

"Point taken." I placed the bottles on the heavy oak table in the middle of the room while Teddy put the screw caps on. She handed one to me and tucked one into her jacket pocket. I did the same.

"Okey dokey, Smokey. Let's roll!"

We headed toward the dividing doorway when I noticed the large, empty dog beds. "Hey, where's your dogs?"

"My hell hounds? They're with Cathy. She needed comfort and protection."

"Your hell...what?" We stepped into the street, Teddy locking the shop door behind us.

"Hell hounds. They belonged to an old boyfriend who was a demon. Alexandra saved me from a pretty horrible situation, actually. She's wonderful." Teddy answered casually as if hell hounds were something you could just pick up at your local shelter.

"Interesting. When I met them, they looked like Bull Mastiffs."

"That's because I glamored them, silly." She smiled, "If you saw what they really looked like...well, you'd have nightmares for a year. I'm used to it, but I can't exactly take them places without their glamor."

I nodded in agreement, because what else could I do? The world Alexandra belonged to, the world I had sworn to obliterate as a Witch Hunter, was all so new to me. I stepped onto the figurative gum and my shoe was now stuck in this world.

But also the Witch Hunter world. If I didn't toe the line and take part in Penny's magic stripping ceremony and her demise on the pyre, I was risking my life and all the witches I was now connected to.

My stomach roiled as we walked up the street and stepped onto the church lawn. I still couldn't think of anything I could do that would get Penny off of the pyre. Literally. I prayed to the Goddess that an idea would strike at just the right time.

Then I realized I had just prayed to the Goddess.

Not the God, not Earl Dagon, and not the demon, Vine.

The Goddess...whomever she may be.

My head spun and my ears rang as we crouched along the edge of the church and peered into the closest windows.

"Blake, look. There's a basket."

I wiggled my fingers in my ears to stop the ringing. This was no time to develop an acute case of tinnitus. I looked in the direction Teddy pointed and saw a good-sized basket holding two bottles of wine. From this angle, I couldn't see into the basket, but had to assume that was the communal basket the demonic nuns would take to the castle for the ceremony to...kill Alexandra.

My stomach roiled again, and the ringing in my ears intensified. This time, I shuffled to the nearest bush and tried to heave quietly. Teddy appeared beside me and rubbed my back.

"I know. It's a lot to take in. There's a lot at stake, Blake. We have to get this done *now*."

I nodded my head and spit.

Darkness was our ally — thank the Goddess — while we slipped to the door, pushing our way inside. Teddy tiptoed animatedly in front of me, toward the basket on the table. "Blake," she whispered, "give me your bottle and keep watch."

I handed her the amber glass full of hope and peered around the corner of the vestibule. "All clear." Teddy pulled the corks from the wine bottles—easy enough to do as they were halfway out already—and poured the contents of the amber glass into them. She topped the bottles with their corks again, lifted the bottles, and gave them a little swirly shake before placing them in the picnic basket.

"Ok, done. Let's get out of here and head to the castle." She kept her voice low. I nodded and moved toward the door.

A muffled sound stopped us in our tracks. We looked at each other, eyebrows knitted together and squinted as if the squinting would assist in the hearing part of the operation. We heard it again. A soft, yet distinct, muffled sound from the room next to the vestibule.

Teddy's eyes grew wide. "Blake, do you think maybe it's Alex?" she mouthed, straining, as I was, to hear the sound again. My heart beat rapidly and I moved toward the door, pressing my ear against it. I heard the muffled sound once more and glanced at Teddy. She motioned for me to open the door. I grabbed the handle, fully expecting it to be locked, but it gave way. My heart beat into my throat as I turned the knob slowly and pushed the door open.

There, bound to a chair and gagged, was the aged Father Donovan. I let out the breath I had been holding and moved toward him. Teddy beat me to him. Yanking at the gag, she released it from his mouth and started on the cord that tied him to the chair.

"Oh, thank the good Lord, you found me." Father Donovan coughed. I quickly peered into the vestibule, hopeful the nuns hadn't heard him, and slid the door shut.

"Oh, Father. Who did this to you?" Teddy asked, then said, "Never mind, I know. We know. About the nuns."

Father Donovan looked us up and down. "You do? I don't understand what's taken over them. They just suddenly appeared that way one day and tied me up!"

"Good Goddess, Father, you've been tied up for days." Teddy finished with the ties and I helped him out of his chair, supporting his weight.

"Well, yes, I mean, they've let me out to the facilities and they've brought food, but otherwise, yes. I don't know what would've happened to me if you hadn't found me."

"I'm afraid you aren't safe yet, Father. We've got to get you out of here."

"But what about the nuns? They need me."

"We're taking care of that, Father. Don't worry," Teddy assured him. "Let's just sneak you out of here."

Holding the Father up with one hand and grasping the door handle with the other, I opened it.

A trio of nuns, with white faces, black eyes, and snarling, gnarled teeth, stood at the door.

My heart leaped. Teddy shrieked. Father Donovan yelled.

The nuns pushed into the room, teeth bared, snapping. I pushed back.

"Teddy, take Father Donovan! Get ready to bolt!" Teddy, smaller than the father but still tough and sturdy, put his arm over her shoulder, tucked to the right side of the room, and got ready.

I moved to the left. "Come get me, *bitches*." The nuns snarled and snapped again and lunged forward. I stepped aside and snapped my arm up, clothes lining them at throat level. They fell back, screeching.

"Teddy, now!" Teddy and Father Donovan bolted out of the room, skirting the nuns where they lay. I jumped over them, nearly falling when one reached out for a shoe and tripped me. I stumbled, but gained my footing and pulled the doors shut behind me. Teddy and Father Donovan were already out the door. Joining them, I asked Father Donovan if he could stand and even walk. He assured me he could.

"Get home, lock yourself in. I don't think the nuns will be an issue after tonight, but lock yourself in, just in case. Call on one of your parishioners if you need help. Can you manage that, Father?"

"Yes, thank you." He nodded and bolted toward the street as if a fire-breathing dragon was after him.

Teddy gave a low whistle as we quickly headed toward Castle Dagon. "The old fella can really move when he wants to...Blake...?"

She turned to face me. Her eyes bulged.

Then everything went black.

TWENTY-NINE

ALEXANDRA

I rattled the cell door.

"Tried that," Penny said as she leaned against the bars of her cell and absently cleaned under her nails.

I took a deep breath and focused my intention on the lock.

"Tried that too. The room is protected, remember? Magic won't work here."

"Well, we have to try *something*, Penny."

Penny was about to toss out a retort when we heard heavy footsteps approaching.

"Think that's the rescue crew?" Penny whispered.

I shook my head. "I don't think so. The footsteps are too heavy. More likely it's the guards, coming to get us for the... ceremony."

"Well, I am waiting for a miracle here, so anytime lover-boy Sherriff wants to step in here is ok with me."

"Miracles are what you make them, Penny."

"Then I guess it's time to make one or kiss my sweet booty goodbye."

Two Witch Hunters, wearing standard-issue brown hooded robes, entered the room.

"Quiet witches! No talking!" One guard shouted. The voice didn't sound at all like Blake's, and my heart sank a little. I peered at the other guard, but could only see his chin. Didn't look like any chiseled chin I knew...

"Who's talking? We weren't talking, were we, Alex? Must be losing your ever-loving minds. Oh, wait. Too late. Or were you even born with minds? How sad for you. You must be an enormous disappointment to your parents..."

"Enough, witch!"

I threw Penny a glance. She defiantly pursed her lips. The quiet guard took the skeleton key out of his robe pocket and unlocked both cells. They each grabbed one of us, gagged us, bound our wrists, and carted us off to the castle courtyard.

My heart beat a funerary tune in time with each step toward our fate. Every step weighed heavily on my heart until we reached the courtyard. I looked around, rapidly moving only my eyes, hoping to see Blake come out of the shadows and save me. Save us. But aside from a circle of hooded hunters, interspersed with the group of demonic nuns, he was nowhere in sight.

Neither was Teddy. Judging from the nun's gnashing teeth and black eyes, Teddy had not yet spiked their wine with her potion. Assuming she could create a potion and spike the nun's wine, to begin with.

And that it worked.

The ceremonial pyre in the center of the courtyard had been built up enough to host two unwilling participants. Penny and me. *Great, just great.*

Any miracle you have, Goddess, now's as good a time as any...

We were shoved in front of the High Commander and listened as the hunters and nuns started their ceremonial chanting. Penny huffed beside me. I glanced at her and she eyed me, bobbing her head up and down and in small circles. For a moment, I couldn't figure out what she was saying. Then it hit me. We were out of the cell room! Our powers would work here! I nodded and focused on the rope holding my wrists together. I could see Penny doing the same.

The rope wouldn't budge.

I frowned at Penny, who mirrored me. I glanced up at a torch secured to one pillar and narrowed my eyes, focusing my intention on the torch. It shifted, the flame snuffing out. One hunter grabbed the torch and relit it.

So, my magic was working, but not on the ropes.

They were protected by...something.

Plus, the two guards hadn't let go of our arms, so, even if I could slip out of the ropes, I couldn't fight off two burly men, let alone an entire circle of them.

We were stuck.

I looked at Penny apologetically. She tipped up one side of her lips, busting out a dimple in a gagged smile, and resignedly shook her head.

I closed my eyes to pray to the Goddess, hoping Penny would understand and do the same.

"Goddess of the night, bring me to the light. Goddess of the day, keep evil away."

I chanted over and over in my head, drawing on the last vestige of power I had.

Hope.

The High Commander raised his hands high in the air. A hush fell around the room. Two hunters carried a wooden podium, placing it in front of the High Commander. Another hunter carried in a large, leather-bound book.

The Book of the Order of the Witch Hunters.

My stomach flipped. They were going to start the power-stripping ceremony. I glanced at Penny. Tear tracks ran down her face and dripped onto her shirt. My chest hurt. I could barely breathe.

This can't be happening.

The ceremony to strip a witch of her powers and burn her at the stake hadn't been performed in over fifty years, and now they were about to strip and burn us both. Black dots swirled in front of my eyes. I squeezed my eyes shut and then opened them again. Not the time to pass out. There just had to be *something* I could do to get us out of this mess. I needed whatever faculties I could muster around me now.

The High Commander summoned the lucky hunter who would receive Penny's powers to stand before him—beside Penny. The hunter gripping my arm pulled me out of the way. I stumbled, but he held me up.

"Hunter, it is your great honor and privilege to strip this witch of her powers and rightfully claim them as your own. What say you?"

The hunter, spoke in a loud, booming voice, "Thanks be to our prominent leader, Earl Dagon, and to Demon Vine. Glory to Dagon! Glory to Vine!"

The hunters in the circle joined in the chant, "Glory to Dagon! Glory to Vine! Glory to Dagon! Glory to Vine!"

Bile swiftly rose in the back of my throat. I swallowed it down in a sharp, painful gulp.

Penny sobbed through her gag, her body shaking.

"Hunter, take a knee," The High Commander continued.

The hunter took a knee.

The hunter grasping Penny's arm shoved her down to her knees without an invitation. Penny landed hard on the stone floor and cried out through her gag. Tears streamed down her face.

The High Commander looked at the book and began the ancient incantation. As he did so, Penny's body rocked, shook, and vibrated out of control. She looked like she was being electrocuted by a cattle prod., he quaked so much.

Then she screamed through the gag. And screamed... and screamed...

I burst forward on shaky legs, but the hunter gripping my arm, pulled me toward him. He bent to my ear and whispered harshly, "You're next, *witch*."

My eyes felt like they were going to pop out of their sockets. *I'm next?* But Blake had told me the hunters weren't allowed to strip my powers, as Earl Dagon had commanded them.

He must have been wrong.

Hope slipped silently away.

I sobbed with my friend.

The High Commander finished the incantation and all at once, a swirl of silver and gold energy flowed from Penny's body. Little silver threads interlaced with sparks spiraled above her head.

Penny slumped to the ground.

The hunters gasped in unison.

The swirl moved from above Penny to just above the receiving hunter. The energy swirled harder and faster, then corkscrewed into the hunter through the top of his head. He let out a mighty roar, his arms, and fingers splayed out on either side of him. The hood of his cloak slid off his head as he raised his eyes to the sky.

It was Jeffrey Deibert, the Mayor!

He'd been a friend of my mother's for years. He'd been over to our house for tea on more occasions than I could count when he was just a city counselor and church member.

And he was a bloody bastard Witch Hunter!

I gaped at him as he writhed, Penny's powers settling into his body and mind. When the last of the energy sunk into him, he stopped writhing and roaring, closed his eyes, and breathed, still perched on one knee.

A loud 'whoop' came from the encircled crowd, including the demonic nuns. I tried to move toward Penny once again, but again, I was held back by the firm grip of the asshole hunter. "It's not over yet, witchy. Now for the fun part..."

I looked up at my hooded captor, shooting him a piercing stare. All I could see was an evil smile beneath the hood. Four hunters grabbed Penny by the upper and lower body and lifted her off the floor. Her head bobbed against the hunter's chest. She was passed out, cold.

Thank the Goddess for small mercies. Maybe she won't come to when they light the pyre.

My blood ran cold as the hunters hoisted Penny up. When they set her down on the pyre, she groggily came to. Looking around the room, then down at herself, she started to shake and scream through the gag. She started beating her feet and legs when the Witch Hunters grasped her by the ankles and wrapped a cord around her legs, completely immobilizing her.

Penny craned her neck back and looked at me. Her eyes were rimmed red and so full of tears and terror, they cut through my heart and soul. At that moment, I'd give anything to switch places with her. Then, as the hunter holding me shoved me in front of the High Commander, I realized switching places was impossible.

It was my turn.

THIRTY

BLAKE

M y body vibrated, but not from the cool chill brushing against my skin. It was something else. I took a breath while my senses started checking off. Head; pounding. Body; laying against something cold. Hands; tied behind me.

My nerves tingled as realization washed over me. Opening my eyes, I was greeted with darkness, but through the darkness, I could make out two shapes. My captors. I peered into the darkness and shifted my head. It pounded again, but I could feel something I couldn't a moment ago. The rough fabric covering my face.

I heard harsh whispering coming from the two figures in front of me. I strained to hear what they were saying, but could not. The hum of tires on pavement drowned out the noise.

I was bound, hooded, and in a van, destination unknown.

THIRTY-ONE

ALEXANDRA

I winced and cried out through the gag as the Witch Hunter grasping my arm, pushed me in front of the High Commander.

"Witch! It is by my Lord Earl Dagon's command that we begin with the ceremonial ritual of stripping you of the evil witch powers you possess and returning them to our great Lord."

I struggled against the gag, pulling away from my captor's grasp. The Commander eyed me, but continued; "The Lord Dagon has sent his sentries, through the guise of these nuns, to perform the task."

With that, the nuns moved forward, moonlight through the courtyard roof reflecting off their stark white faces enough that I had to narrow my eyes from the harsh light.

This could not be happening.

Confusion, mixed with fear, mixed with reality settled deep into my bones. Blake told me the hunters had strict instructions not to mess with my powers, but that didn't mean the nuns did.

And they have every intention of stripping my Goddess-given powers and burning me beside my best friend.

I struggled some more, the sharp sting of tears blurring my vision. Another Witch Hunter joined the party to my left and grabbed my free arm. I was pinned between two burly assholes with nowhere to go.

It was no use.

I was losing my powers...and my life.

A larger, taller nun stepped forward and retrieved some items from a nearby basket. She was preparing for their communion! I prayed to the Goddess that Teddy had spiked their wine and that the effect would take hold sooner than later. I watched as the nuns took their communion, their leader pouring wine into small chalices and passing them out to the nuns, who dipped their communal wafers into the wine and wasted no time in devouring the same. Trickles of wine and wafers littered their faces and snagged teeth as they stared in my direction, their eyes boring into me.

I felt naked and terrified. But if I felt a sense of nakedness now, I could only imagine what I would feel when the ritual was over. I glanced behind one shoulder to Penny on the pyre, and she met my eyes with the same desperation that wracked my body. I looked around the room at the hooded figures, but they all stood where they had been through the first ritual, only their chins exposed under the large hoods, and none of them looked like Blake.

The nuns circled me. When they closed the loop, my two captors let go of my arms and returned to their place in the outer circle to bear witness to my demise.

Like one big, happy, freaking demonic family.

The nuns started swaying back and forth in unison, chanting the ritual chant in the ancient language. The language of the Demon Vine, written into a book, at the bequest of Earl Dagon.

My ancestor.

Whose blood ran through my veins.

Whose powers I possessed, as the last of his line.

Whose...powers....I...possessed... A flood of hot relief hit my heart. His powers! I was a Dagon! If I could activate my powers, maybe I could control—I screamed through the gag. A searing feeling cut through me like a blade made of the sharpest steel, and I screamed again. The gag vomited from my mouth and fell in a bile—riddled pool at the head nun's feet.

I filled my lungs with fresh air and let another scream rip through me.

The pain was nothing I'd ever felt before. It sliced through me, cutting me to ribbons from the inside out. I gasped, raking fresh air into my lungs, but only jagged bits of air crept in. My heart was bursting through my chest and my lungs had no way of coming to its aid. I was drowning like a fish freshly torn from the sea.

A swirl of energy, much like the one I had seen above Penny's head, formed, shaping an umbilical cord, one end attached to my body and the other rising higher and higher, into the night sky, toward the Earl, toward the Demon Vine, or maybe just toward nothing and nowhere.

The last piece of my energy tore away from my body in a last scream and a flailing swoop into the starry night.

Then, nothing.

The hunters cheered and took a knee, whooping praise to Earl Dagon and Demon Vine in unison. The nuns stared into the night sky, raising their arms above them and sending their final chants into the abyss before lowering their arms and looking down on me, lying in a puddle of my sick, completely drained of energy and...my magic.

My breath came in raspy gasps as the nuns moved back, surrounding the pyre I would soon lie on, ensuring they had the best view. Four hunters grabbed me, hastily pulling me off the floor and easily tossing me onto the pyre, my head at Penny's feet, her head at mine.

They bound my feet with cord, as they had Penny's, but neither of us was bound *to* the pyre. We didn't have to be, our bindings were so tight, the only way we could get off was to roll off the pyre. That would be useless, the hunters would just throw us back on. There *had* to be another way.

I lay there, praying to the Goddess while scanning my body from head to toe. An emptiness crept over me. I was devoid of my lifeline, my powers.

Except...

I whipped my head up and looked at Penny. Her body was heaving with sobs. She had pushed the gag from her mouth, but no words escaped her lips. I opened my eyes wide and nodded toward her. She stopped, sniffed, and peered at me, but it was no use. She could no longer sense what I was thinking. That ability had been torn from her, along with the rest.

"I still have powers," I mouthed. Penny's eyes grew wide, her mouth gaped open.

"What? How?" she mouthed back.

"Watch." That was all I said.

The High Commander began reading from the book again. Something about bearing witness to the sacrifice they were about to make for the sake of their Earl, blah blah, yada yada. Shit like that.

I wasn't listening.

I stared up at the stars, closed my eyes, and summoned the deepest, darkest part of me. The part that I had kept hidden for so long. The part that I had rejected, loathed, and despised was now my only hope.

They may have taken *my* magic, but they couldn't take my ancestral, evil Dagon blood.

I focused on my anger, funneling it into the core of my being. I thought of the injustice—of every injustice—the Witch Hunters had thrust upon *my kindred for four hundred long years.*

My hands, still tied behind my back, tingled with hot, fiery heat. I pushed my feet onto the pyre and raised my butt into a high bridge position to avoid burning my back. As soon as I felt the cords fall away from my wrists, I sat up and pulled at the cords on my feet. They were too tight, so I pointed one finger at them. A red flame, much different from the heat of my witchy power, shot toward the cords binding my ankles and they disintegrated.

I quickly stood. The gaping crowd gasped in unison. Many of the hunters pulled their hoods from their heads, exposing themselves. I recognized almost every one of them. *Bastards.* I turned and faced the High Commander. His hood was also pushed off his head. It was Sherriff Roberts! *Bloody bastard!* His dark skin tinged an angry red.

"Hunters! Capture that witch. Tie her down to the pyre *now!*"

It was my time to shine.

Several of the hunters broke their circle and pushed past the nuns, who now looked a lot less like demonic freaks and more like the gentle, kind nuns I grew up with. The shock on their faces was clear that they had no clue what was going on or how they got there. Whatever demonic presence that had a hold of them was gone. I said a silent 'hooray' for Teddy. Her potion worked, but too late to save my witchy powers.

The Witch Hunters rushed toward the pyre. Jagged bursts of red-hot heat flared from my fingertips, carrying whips of dark red flames with them. I spread my arms wide and splayed my fingers, the zig-zagging bursts of red electric energy licking hungrily at the air.

"Don't come any closer."

They stopped. One of them yelled, "Her magic still holds, Commander. The ritual didn't work!" It was Jeremy, my favorite Starbucks barista.

Utterly disappointing. Where was I gonna go for a decent caramel macchiato now?

The Sherriff abandoned the Book and moved toward the pyre.

"Witch! What magic is this?"

"The Dagon kind."

I focused the energy on the palms of my hands. The deep, red energy balls grew larger the more I summoned. I looked toward the nuns, now cowering, huddled behind a pillar. "Sister Mary!" I called to the head of the Order. She whipped her head my way. "Quick! Leave! NOW!" She didn't hesitate to lead the group of eighteen from the courtyard and out of the castle.

I turned toward the Sherriff. "Call off your dogs and release Penny. Now, *Commander*." I glanced at Pen. Her eyes glistened, her smile as wide as her delightful booty—and heart.

I refused to let her die.

"I will not, *witch*. Who are you to give me a command?"

"You know who I am, Sherriff. The last of Earl Dagon's bloodline."

"The Earl has commanded this ritual, witch. He has

summoned you to join him and his bride. We are following his orders!"

"The Earl can *suck it*, and so can you!" I threw an intense ball of flame toward a pillar next to the Sherriff, punching a large dent in the stone.

"Atta witch! Give 'em hell, Alex! Woo! You're in trouble now, *boys!*" Penny called out.

Careful to keep the energy balls from crumbling the surrounding courtyard, I threw a second ball toward a statue in the corner, obliterating it, and then at a fountain in another corner. Water, stone, and flames shot up and out, hitting the hunters, knocking some of them off their feet, and drenching others. Witch Hunters started running in every direction, yelling for someone to *do something*.

I did something.

I used the energy spikes from one finger to dissolve Penny's bindings. As I was helping her off the pyre, two Witch Hunters grabbed me from behind, holding my arms and pulling me back. Immediately, balls of intense heat burst from my hands. "Penny, look out!" Penny dove to one side as I 'tossed' the fireballs onto the pyre. The dry wood quickly ignited, burning through the pyre in a matter of seconds. I ignited my hands once again and looked at the hunters on either side of me.

"Wanna be next, boys?"

The hunters released me and ran toward the exit, yelling; "*Not worth it...*"

I smiled but held the flame.

Penny turned in circles. "The room is clearing out fast, Alex. It's like they just got a whiff of a Blackjack fart."

I laughed, a jolt of adrenaline and joy bursting through my body. I looked around.

Sherriff Gordon and a handful of hunters remained.

Walking toward him, flames from my hands still licking the air, he backed away, taking his place behind the book.

"You can strip my Goddess powers, Sherriff, but you can't take my ancestral, Dagon blood."

A voice came from somewhere above or behind me.

"That is correct, my love."

I whipped my head around to find its source. Penny, the hunters, and the Commander did the same. A stream of red vapors appeared in the center of the courtyard. The vapors became increasingly solid in form until a clear, gauzy, unmistakable shape formed.

Earl Dagon.

The heat from my hands extinguished. I dropped my arms to my sides, my chin hanging low enough to catch a dozen flies. Penny grasped one of my hands and held firm. A unanimous thud came from the circle of hunters as they immediately took a knee, bowing to their dead Earl.

"I commend thee, my love, for harnessing your special powers. They are yours to keep while you claim your ancestral throne in Castle Dagon."

"Huh?" I'd lost all my senses and my intelligence. Gaping at the apparition of my ancestor—and former lover from another life—I shuddered.

The Earl chuckled. *"It's all according to plan, my love. On the night of Samhain—your 38th birthday you would be availed of your useless witchy powers and take the throne as my last remaining heir."*

"You've *got* to be kidding me! You *planned* this?"

"I do not jest, my love. Indeed, this has been my plan all along."

"But...I don't *want* it..." I could barely form a word, let alone an intelligent sentence.

The ghostly Earl walked directly in front of me.

Touching my face with his hands, a tingly, cold sensation whipped through me.

"You want it, my love. And you will take it. It's my ultimate gift to you. You may have refused me in life, but you will not refuse this. I never stopped loving you." He bent his head toward mine.

Was he *seriously* about to kiss me right now?

I shuttered and tucked my lips, forming a thin line. He kissed me anyway. I was instantly disgusted at the pull in my loins. Was I that desperate for a man that I could be attracted to a dead Earl? I pulled away, as did the Earl.

He thankfully turned his attention to the Witch Hunters. The High Commander closed his own gaping maw and took a knee. The Witch Hunters who stayed for the afterparty did as well. Penny sucked in a breath beside me.

"All hail your new Queen!" The Earl commanded.

"Hail to the Queen! Hail to the Queen! Hail to the Queen!" Rose from the crowd.

A low whistle escaped Penny's lips. "Wow, Alex. You're kind of a big deal. You still wanna be friends? I mean, I'm just a lowly subject...Also, happy birthday to you..." Penny sing-songed.

I spun in a slow circle in the center of the courtyard as the Witch Hunters bowed and hailed. This was a gift that I hadn't expected and wasn't really sure I wanted, but we were alive so...

"Happy birthday to me..."

THIRTY-TWO

BLAKE

My body rolled and bounced in the back of the van for what seemed like hours after coming to. Cruising along a dirt road at highway speeds, every muscle in my body hurt from the ride. I was fully aware of my surroundings, but, because of the hood over my head, couldn't see.

I tried moving my legs, but my ankles were also bound. I couldn't really tell if Teddy was in the van beside me, but heard nothing as I strained to hear her breathing or movement. A fleeting wave of relief flushed through me. Whoever they were, they weren't after Teddy; they were only after me. It was the who, what, and why that eluded me.

I had to assume it wasn't a Witch Hunter, but, thinking that through, I couldn't deny the possibility either. I wasn't exactly careful about hiding the time I'd spent with Alexandra, and if the hunters suspected me of taking her side, well, doing so was a punishable offense.

My captors rarely spoke to one another and when they did, their tones were undiscernable. Thankful for the small mercy of no gag, I contemplated calling out to them but thought it would be better to play the part of a coma patient and just lie still.

I formed a plan.

When we stopped, hopefully soon, my captors would likely drag me out of the van and take me...somewhere. Hopefully, in the time it took them to do that, the opportunity to fight for my life would present itself.

Hopefully...

THIRTY-THREE

ALEXANDRA

"Okay, okay, that's enough. Stand up for Goddess' sake and stop that chanting." The Witch Hunters did as I commanded.

"Impressive..." Penny whispered beside me. "Make them dance a jig now, will you? No?"

I shook my head and stifled a giggle. Turning to Sherriff Roberts, I said, "Sherriff, perform the incantation that gives us our powers back." I paused for a moment, then thought, *why the heck not?* "I command you."

Penny snorted beside me. "Yeah. You heard the Queen. Get on with it." Penny walked up to Mayor Deibert and repeatedly poked his chest with a finger. "Give. Me. My. Powers. Back. You. Witch. Hating. Asshole!"

The Mayor held his hands up and spread his fingers. "If there is such an incantation, we don't know it."

My stomach hit the floor. "What? What do you mean? There's got to be a spell."

Sherriff Roberts spoke up. "I'm so sorry, my Queen, but

we have only been taught the removal spell. Once that is complete, the witch is ceremoniously burned on the pyre. A reversal spell has never been needed."

"Holy crap on a cracker. You're kidding." Penny voiced what I'd been thinking.

The Sherriff shook his head. "I'm sorry, my Queen, but that's all we know. That's all that we have been taught from the book."

The book!

I strode to the podium and flipped through the ancient text. "The symbols and writing look so similar from page to page. Are you sure there's no instruction here?"

"There may well be, but we have only ever been taught —and passed down—the ritual we performed this evening."

I looked up at the starry sky and sighed. "Is there anyone who can interpret this thing?"

"Not that we know of, my Queen. So much of that knowledge has died with the aging hunters. We haven't had a ritual in well over fifty years. Many of the elders have taken the knowledge of the ancient language to their graves." Sherriff Roberts looked at me, sheepishly. "I'm sorry, your Grace."

Frustration rumbled through me, igniting the Dagon heat in my hands. I looked down at my red palms, then up at the Sherriff and Mayor. They took a step back. *Tempting.* Now that my witch powers were gone, the Dagon ones were more than ready to lash out.

I'd have to keep my anger in check.

"Thank you, Sherriff. You and I can discuss this further another time. For now, I'm taking the book with me. You and your men are dismissed."

"Yes, your Grace."

"Oh, and Sherriff?"

"Yes, your Grace?"

"Make it clear to all that the hunt for witches is officially *off*."

The Sherriff stared at me, wide-eyed. A rejoicing 'whoop' came from Penny and one hunter. Everyone turned to look toward the holler, but it wasn't clear who made it.

"Yes...your Grace...I...I will send the news of your reign to the World-Wide Order of the Witch Hunters."

"Very good. You may go." I pointed toward the entrance. The hunters followed each other and left in silence.

"I have to admit, that was kinda fun," I whispered to Penny, who was nodding at the speed of a bobblehead on a car dash.

One hunter remained. "Oh my gosh, Alex. That was amazing. You're the gosh darn Queen," his masculine voice boomed through the courtyard. I stared at him for a moment. It wasn't Blake, but I didn't recognize him, either. Penny and I looked at each other, then back at the hunter. Realization dawned.

"Teddy?" Penny and I asked in unison.

"Oh, jolly ranchers, yes, it's me." Teddy shed the glamor and appeared as her true self, with simple hair and makeup, her tattoos gone. A huge smile fixed on her sweet face.

"Teddy!" I hugged her. Penny joined us for a much-needed, much-deserved group hug. "You're ok, thank the Goddess. Great job with the potion."

"Thanks. So super stoked it worked. I only wish it worked sooner. Maybe you'd still have your powers..." Teddy looked down at her boots.

"Hey, it's okay, Teddy. You did your best. We'll get our powers back, one way or another." I gave her a quick squeeze. "Do you have any idea where Blake is?"

Teddy's words flowed in a rush. "Well, yes, and no. He *was* with me. He came to the shop, and we realized you'd been kidnapped. We finished the potion and spiked the nun's wine. When we were heading to the castle, someone —a couple of people, I think—came up behind us and knocked us out. I woke up on the grass with Blackjack licking my face. Blake was gone."

"I got there just in time to see two people tie him up and throw him in a van. I thought about attacking them, but, well, if something were to happen to me, *then you'd really be up poopy creek."*

"Blackjack!" He had come out from behind Teddy and peered up at me. He must have been hiding under her robes. I picked him up and squeezed him. "I'm so happy to be alive and squeeze you again."

"Me too. My turn." Penny grabbed Blackjack from my arms and squished him.

"Oomph! Call off your minion, woman."

I laughed. "Can you believe what happened here tonight?" The three of them shook their heads.

"It's one for the *her*story books, for sure," Penny nodded. "I just wish we could figure out how to get our powers back."

"And find Blake."

"Sure. However, powers are higher on my personal list of wants. That and getting home to my wife. Sorry lover-girl."

I nodded my head. "Yeah, I can agree with that. Kinda hard to find him without them, and I know Cathy is beside herself with worry."

Teddy piped up, "Maybe your *new* powers would work to find him?"

I considered this for a moment, then shrugged, "I have

no clue what the Dagon powers are capable of, other than destruction. I guess I could find out. Or get the book interpreted..."

"Orrrrr," Penny tapped a finger on her forehead. "We summon Cressy and see what he knows and if *he* can get our powers back!"

"Great idea!" Teddy and I agreed. "Let's do it!"

"Ahem. I hate to be the smartest cat in the room but, since I usually am, I'll remind you that you have no powers to summon the man with!"

"Shoot, you're right, Blackjack."

"What did the cool cat say?" Penny asked.

"He told me he's the smartest cat in the room and reminded me we have no powers to summon Cressy with."

"Oh. Right. Teensy snag." Penny pinched two fingers together.

Teddy piped up. "What about me? Could I summon Cressy?"

I clapped my hands. "Yes, of course, you could. With Blackjack."

"Right," Penny agreed. "Sorry, Blackjack, guess you're not the smartest kitty in the room this time." Penny gave him another squeeze. He pulled back and looked at me.

"Fine, I'll give the red-headed weirdo this one."

I laughed. "Ok, let's stop wasting time and get to work!"

"Where should we do this here?" Teddy asked.

"It's as good a place as any, sure." I nodded.

Penny snorted. "Ya, here is good. Besides, Alex owns the place now. Her crazy, demon-loving ex left it to her. Perhaps you've met him? A real deadbeat. HA!" She snorted again. "*Dead*beat—get it? HA!" She slapped a knee. Teddy and I couldn't help but join in her laughter.

THIRTY-FOUR

ALEXANDRA

"*Heaven to Earth, hear my plea, bring back he who watches over me. Goddess and Gods of North, East, South, West, allow us to commune with our dear Cress.*"

The torches flame flickered with the swirl of Cressy's entrance. We had set up the courtyard as best we could with the limited supplies we could find to welcome him. Penny found a bottle of salt in the museum's staff room and poured a scant circle. We lit some candles that we found in the dusty bedrooms, but the torches were the main flame and lit up the otherwise dark, open-air courtyard. We couldn't find any herbs but hoped for the best.

Cressy's essence swirled and gathered into his dashing form. He glanced around the courtyard, at the ash from the burned pyre, at our feet, then at us.

"Alexandra, why are we in Castle Dagon's courtyard?"

Teddy, Penny, and I started giggling. Our girlish giggles

turned into hoots of laughter. "Oh, Cressy, you won't believe what we've been through."

"I have time, dear girl. Why don't you tell me?"

I told him. Cressy's face was a mix of concern, alarm, inquisitiveness, and joy as I told him about the day.

A low whistle escaped his lips as I finished. "Alexandra, what an unbelievable turn of events. This is more than I could have ever dreamed, my dear girl. *You are the Queen of the Order of the Witch Hunters.* Absolutely phenomenal." Cressy gathered me into his ghostly embrace across the salty threshold. I reveled in his warm embrace and could still smell his marvelous aftershave.

"You should have seen her, Cressy," Penny piped up. "She was a real bitch, witch. Telling those hunters exactly where to go and what to do. It was incredible."

Cressy laughed. "I'm sure she was amazing." He looked down at me, beaming. My heart burst. Cressy was my substitute father. Making him proud was so important to me. My smile slightly faded. I fleetingly wished my mother could be here, but knew she wouldn't have reacted the same way.

She spent most of my youth reprimanding me for who I was and trying to hide the fact that her daughter was a witch. Now, as an adult, I understood it was because she was afraid for my life, but I had no clue why she was so abusive to me as a child.

I shook off the sinking feeling. Lifting my eyes to meet Cressy's, I thanked him. "I appreciate your support, Cress, but getting our power back is pretty front-and-center. Also, finding Blake."

"Right, yes. That," Penny injected.

"Ahh, yes. That." Cressy agreed. "We'll get to that in a moment. First, a warning."

"A *warning*?"

"Yes, my dear. You've made amazing strides today both in freeing yourself from Dagon's dreams and having power over the hunters, but I wouldn't sleep without locking your doors and setting your house alarm just yet."

"What do you mean, Cress? You think I'm in danger?"

"Well, there will be those hunters who won't agree or accept your new position, Alexandra. I'm just saying—be careful. Don't turn your back on anyone. And don't trust anyone just yet."

I considered Cressy's words carefully. "Makes sense, I guess. But it's not like I can't defend myself." I looked down at my hands and a small, red-flamed fireball appeared in my palms.

"Just be careful, my dear. Learn to harness the powers and use them in the right way. Something I regretfully couldn't teach you when I was alive. I was too busy trying to teach you to keep those powers under wraps."

I nodded my head and closed my fists, snuffing out the flames. "I understand, Cress, and I promise I'll be careful. What about my witch powers? Can you help us get them back?"

Cressy looked from me to Penny and back again, shaking his head. "I'm afraid it's not as simple as a snap of my fingers, ladies."

The sinking feeling in my belly returned. "What do you mean, Cress?"

"Well, I believe the High Commander when he said he didn't know the spell to return your powers. There's never been a case of giving a witch her powers back once they've been stripped...and..."

"And...?"

"I don't have the power to overrule the hunter's ritual."

Penny's jaw dropped to the floor, as did mine. "Excuse me? What's that now? How could that be, Cressy?" Penny's voice went from whiny child to quiet as a mouse.

"Cressy, can't you do anything?" I asked.

"Not without interpreting the Witch Hunters book. The answers, hopefully, are in there."

"We could probably figure out the book, but the Sherriff said they don't know if there even *is* a way."

"Yeah," Penny thrust her hands on her hips. "What if there *isn't one*?"

"Let's not assume, ladies. Focus on having that book interpreted."

I paced the salt circle around Cressy's ghostly form. "We'll need one of the elder hunters, according to Sherriff Roberts. He said the ability to interpret the book is dying off with the elders."

"That makes sense, of course." Cressy agreed. "Since the witch community went 'underground' nearly...goodness, sixty or seventy years ago...the Order of the Witch Hunters assumed they had wiped the witch race from the face of the earth, so there really hasn't been a need for interpretation of the book, and no need to pass the knowledge down."

Penny snorted. "Arrogant bastards, thinking they'd wiped us out. We showed them."

"Yeah," Teddy piped up, pumping a fist in the air. "And now one of *our kind* is in charge."

The two witches started doing some weird secret handshake thing that neither one of them knew how to do, making it up on the fly. This resulted in more face and body slapping than necessary, and a lot of cackling laughter. I had to join in. The laughter, not the slapping.

"Alexandra, it may be useful for you to use your new power as the Hunter Queen and call in the elders."

"Yes, Cressy, I was just thinking that, actually. But also, finding Blake."

The slap-happy duo stopped mid-slap and looked at me.

"Can you find out where he is, Cress?" Penny asked.

"I can try, of course." He slipped a ghostly finger under my chin and tilted my head up to meet his eyes. "I know you have feelings for Blake, Alexandra, but I implore you to be careful. He's still a Witch Hunter and can be influenced to work against you."

I lowered my gaze from Cressy's eyes to his very fine smoking jacket. "I promise, Cressy."

"Very good. Alright, give me a moment. I'll see what I can find out."

Cressy's essence flew into a funnel in the center of the circle. The three of us watched. When he returned to form, his brow furrowed as he looked at me. My heart sank right into my shoes.

"You couldn't find him?"

Cressy shook his head. "No, which could only mean one of two things. One, he's protected by magic, or two..."

"He's dead."

THIRTY-FIVE

BLAKE

The van rumbled to a stop, and two occupants in the van's front got out. The sliding side door opened with the slight squeal of rusty bearings. One of my captors, I think the passenger, moved into the van and grabbed hold of my feet. I was tempted to kick, but thought I should wait until I was outside the van, or until they released my bindings—assuming they would. Then I could overtake my captors and escape in the van.

Neither one of them seemed to be any bigger than me. This should be easy.

The larger of the two grabbed my shoulders and together they moved me out of the van and into...a chair. They bound me *to* it.

Dammit.

The thought of escape dashed with the tightening of the new bindings. I briefly wondered, yet again, what I'd done to deserve to be captured, and what lay ahead. Beads of sweat pebbled my brow under the coarse linen hood. My mind dashed around scenarios of torture and fighting to the end of my life from a single bullet.

Then to Alexandra.

Her beautiful face, her perfect lips, the kiss we shared. A burning in my belly forced my resolve. I *had* to escape. *I had to be with Alexandra.*

One captor leaned over both sides of the chair and clicked something into place. They moved me, and the chair —a wheelchair—toward a large, dark shape. The other captor walked ahead and opened a door into the dark shape —a building. I couldn't see any details through the rough fabric of my hood. All of my other senses, however, were alive and in tune.

When we entered, a comforting blanket of warm air surrounded my aching body. The aromatic scent of sandalwood and roses hit me and I breathed deeply, reminding me of something I couldn't quite put my finger on. The roses, of Alexandra's perfume, but it was more than that. Something scratched at the back of my memory banks but wouldn't come forward.

Another door opened, and I was wheeled in. The door closed behind us. This room smelled like fuel oil...a garage?

A bright light flickered and blazed just over my head. Even with the hood on, I squinted from the light.

One captor stepped over to me, sliding the hood from my head, then stepped back, hiding behind the bright light.

I blinked rapidly, adjusting to the light. Squinting, I peered into the room at the two dark figures. Despite the light, my eyes opened wide as my stomach hit the floor.

Oh, my God...

THIRTY-SIX

ALEXANDRA

It had been days of solace and frustration since communing with Cressy and taking over the Dagon throne. Blake was still missing. I could barely eat. Foamy coffee in the morning and a good dose of red wine in the evening were my primary source of nutrients.

The day after the ritual, I asked Teddy to scry the map for Blake's location, hoping her somewhat juvenile powers would lead us right to him, but the pendulum and the Ouija board yielded no results. My already knotted belly tightened even further. Cressy's words ran an endless loop through my brain. It could mean that Blake's location was protected by magic, like the Dagon Dungeon cells, or...

He's dead.

No! I'd shake my head and let my frustrations fly with my coffee cup against the tile floor of my kitchen or my wine glass into the fireplace. At this rate, I'd have to replace my cups and glasses before the week's end.

The hollow feeling in my chest and belly since losing

my powers and Blake kept me trapped in the comfort of my home. After Blackjack's Oscar-worthy performance highlighting my need for a shower and deodorant, I got ready and went to meet with Sherriff Roberts. When I entered the building and walked through the bullpen to his office, all the deputies stopped what they were doing, got off their seats, and took a knee.

Of *course*, they were all Witch Hunters.

What better position to investigate witch claims than a cop? I stopped in the middle of the room and turned in a circle. Every head was bowed, so I couldn't meet anyone's eyes and see either their admiration or their distaste. Cressy's warning to watch my back rippled through me, punctuated by tiny gooseflesh.

"At ease, boys." I walked confidently to Sherriff Robert's office, opened the door without invitation—because why not—and took a seat in the chair across from his desk. The Sherriff quickly hung up the phone mid-sentence, and without warning whoever was on the other end. He slid from his chair and was about to take a knee when I held up a hand.

"Please, just sit, for the Goddess's sake."

"Your Grace. What a pleasure to see you." He smiled, but I narrowed my eyes at him. Was he faking it, or genuinely happy? I had to assume faking it, again, Cressy's words resonating.

I got right to the point. "Where's Blake Sheraton?"

The Sherrif's face twisted into concern. "We really don't know, your Grace. But we are all working on finding him now."

Again, I narrowed my eyes, trying to sense whether he was telling the truth. Everything was bloody difficult without my powers to back me up. "No progress? You really don't know where he is?" I paused for a moment, then thought, what the hell? "Your Queen commands the truth, Sherriff." I opened one hand wide to conjure a red Dagon fireball, but the Sherriff answered quickly, saving me the trouble.

Gordon nodded rapidly. "And the truth is what I give you, your Grace. Nobody knows who took him or where he may be. I'm sorry."

I let out a frustrated breath. "Could any of the other Witch Hunters have taken him...that night?" I faltered, thinking about the near escape from the castle pyre. One thing I could grudgingly thank my Dagon powers for. *My life*.

"Absolutely not, your Grace. All the hunters were in attendance that night. Being it was the first...well...ritual in years of...some significance, they all wanted to be in attendance."

A streak of frustrated heat burned a spot in my palms. I clenched my fists, willing the flame away.

"Fine. But finding him is your top priority, got it? Unless there's a life-or-death situation in Castle Point to attend to, Blake Sheraton is to be found. Clear?"

"Very clear, yes, your Grace."

"Good. Now. I want to assemble the elder Witch Hunters to interpret the book. We want our powers back."

The Sherriff paused, his eyes flitting from me to the window and around the room.

"Is there a problem, Gordon?"

"N—no, your Grace. It's just that there are so few...and most of them infirm..."

"Not my problem. There's a world of them out there, Gordon. Find one, find ten, just find the ones that are still well enough to interpret that damn book!"

"Yes, your Grace."

With that, I stormed out of the building, rolling my eyes as the hunters—deputies—shot from their desks to take a knee.

This Queen thing was already exhausting.

Sitting on the back porch of my home on Ocean View Drive, I sipped my frothy cappuccino and watched two butterflies duke it out in front of me. My morning coffee foam art, meant to be a heart, looked more like a blob of mud, summing up my life.

No powers.

No Blake.

No reason.

Even the butterflies gave up their fight and landed on a flower.

"Yoo-hoo, you back here?" Penny, Cathy, Teddy, and her hounds appeared around the corner of the house. Blackjack leaped from where he lay in a sunbeam, barely touched the porch, and skidded to a tree as the hounds bounded over to me, lapping at my hands and face. I rubbed their heads and cooed at them, a welcome distraction from my darkening thoughts.

"Hey, lady. We've been knocking at the door for like, a hot minute." Penny, her arm around her beaming wife, stepped onto the porch and sat on the porch swing with Cathy. Teddy took a chair and snapped her fingers. The hounds pulled back from me and immediately lay at her feet.

"Sorry, I didn't hear you. Kinda lost in thought."

"Moping over the hot Sherriff, more like it," Penny guffawed.

Cathy elbowed her and pouted. "I'm so sorry, Alex. You've had no luck with the search?"

I shook my head. "No, and Sherriff Roberts hasn't produced a single living hunter who can interpret the book, either."

"I'm so super sorry, Alex. I've been working on scrying the map every day, but the pendulum still doesn't swing for me." Teddy pooched her bottom lip. "I'm not powerful enough, I guess."

I patted her hand. "Teddy, that's not true. You're plenty powerful. More than likely, it's like Cressy said. He is either protected by magic or..." I couldn't finish the sentence.

"Don't go there, woman, not again, please. I can't take any more of your simpering over the baboon and I'm tiring of pussyfooting over broken glass." Blackjack had snuck from the tree onto the porch and jumped on my lap.

"Sorry, Blackjack. I've been a real Debbie Downer lately."

"No arguments here."

"Understandable, Alex." Penny injected as if hearing Blackjack's voice. "We've been through a lot the past few days. But we're *alive*. Try to focus on that, huh?" She squeezed Cathy.

I forced a smile. It was wonderful to see them reunited and happy, despite Penny losing her powers. I was beginning to think she was okay with not having any. She and Cathy were now truly equals. For a moment, I wished I could be okay with losing my own powers, but I really couldn't. Having only the Dagon powers at my disposal didn't do me an ounce of good for finding Blake. They were clearly meant for destruction and evil, not good.

Blake was good.

And, deep in my heart, I just *had* to believe that he was alive and okay.

"Hey!" Penny piped up. "Why don't we get outta Dodge

for a day and go visit your mom? You haven't seen her in weeks. We could make it a fun road trip! Whad'ya say, *Queen*?"

I rolled my eyes, but a smile pulled at my lips. "Yeah, good idea Pen. I just wish we had our powers. Maybe then the three of us could force the demon's hex from her..."

Teddy shot up out of her chair and started dancing around.

"Bug crawl up your undies, Ted?" Penny laughed.

"No! Better."

"What could be better than ants in your pants? A frog in your dog? A jig in your pig? A—oomph!" Cathy's elbow met Penny's stomach.

"What's up, Teddy?" I laughed.

"The potion! I still have some bottled up from the batch we fed the nuns. It worked to release them from the demon's grasp..."

Penny's eyes grew as wide as I'm sure my own had. Even without our powers, we knew what each other was thinking.

Perhaps, if it worked for the nuns, it would work for Mom!

"Teddy, that's brilliant!" I clapped.

"It's settled then. We go. I'll bring the road snacks."

"I call shotgun," Teddy squealed. Penny stood up and started dancing a gig with Teddy around the porch. Cathy's laughter resounded with my own, as we watched the Goddess-awful performance.

A tiny spark of hope ignited my heart, burning away the darkness.

THIRTY-SEVEN

BLAKE

N*o way.*
It just couldn't be.
Could it?

I stared at my captors past the beams of bright light from the lamp overhead. The air left my lungs despite my chin hitting my chest. Darks dots peppered my eyesight. I forced air into my lungs. My entire body tingled and vibrated with cold anticipation. I moved my tongue around my mouth, conjuring enough saliva to speak.

"...Mom? ...Dad?"

"Hello, son."

THIRTY-EIGHT

ALEXANDRA

The four of us, myself, Teddy, Penny, and Cathy, made the most of the road trip to Lexington County Sanatarium to visit my mom. Teddy held a vial of the precious potion in her hands the entire trip, barely letting go to grab a snack from the many options Penny brought.

Excited anticipation bubbled inside me. My logical mind said I shouldn't get my hopes up, that Mom will probably not come out from under the demon's curse, but my heart wanted to hold on to any fragment of hope it could grasp.

When we arrived and shuffled into Mom's room, she was at her usual post, sitting in a wheelchair, staring out the window at nothing. A little jolt of joy zipped through me when I realized I couldn't see the swarm of black sentry flies above her head. Maybe the curse had lifted? I kneeled in front of her and tried to capture her eyes.

"Hi, Mom. How are you?" Her eyes remained stone cold and staring. My heart sank. She was completely unchanged since my last visit, which meant the flies had to still be there, but I couldn't see them without my powers.

"Teddy, can you see a swarm of flies above my mom's head?"

Teddy quirked an eyebrow at me. "Flies? Like, actual annoying buzz-buzz black things?"

"Yeah. They're sentries of the demon who hexed my mom. I can't see them without my powers. Can you try?"

Teddy squinted into the sunlight flowing through the window over Mom's head. Frowning, she took several steps back, out of the sunlit path. Her eyes grew wide. Slowly, from toes to purple pigtails, she wiggled.

"Oh. My. Goddess. I see a dark, swarming cloud above her head. I can't tell if there are flies in the cloud or not. It's just a hazy mess. A kind of funnel—type thing. Could that be them?"

Penny scooted over to high-five Teddy, then slapped her tiny rump. "Yeah, witchy sista. You got it!" Teddy wiggled some more. I couldn't help but laugh.

"Gosh, that's amazing. I can't see a thing." Cathy stepped back beside Teddy and peered in the same direction, then shrugged.

Penny slid an arm around her wife's waist and nodded her head. "I know how you feel, babe. I got nothin'."

"That's great Teddy. So, we know the curse is still there. Penny, grab that juice glass. Let's try to get some of that potion into Mom."

I watched as Teddy ever-so-carefully un-cork the vial and poured some of the precious potion into the glass Penny was holding, corking it just as carefully when done.

Penny held the glass with two hands and carefully stepped slowly toward me, passing me the glass. She bowed, stretching out her arms with the glass out to me. I took it, giggling a little at my two goofy companions.

"Here Mom, try a little of this, will you?" I placed the glass on Mom's lips and tipped it. Still staring straight ahead, she opened her mouth slightly, allowing a generous amount of liquid to fall in. I pulled the half-empty glass away from her lips and wiped her chin with a nearby tissue, watching her throat work as she swallowed the liquid. Assuming the potion tasted as bad as it smelled, she swallowed it down without making a face.

The four of us stood back, barely blinking our eyes or breathing, waiting for some type of reaction.

Finally, it came.

Mom's eyes started blinking rapidly. She took a deep breath and started looking around the room. My heart and the lump in my throat pulsed in rhythm as I watched my Mom, in a demonic coma for the past twenty years, 'wake up.' She turned her head toward me.

"Alexandra?" she whispered.

"Mom!" I rushed to kneel in front of her, a steady stream of tears tickling my cheeks. "Can you hear me? Can you—"

"Oh, Alexandra, you must hurry. Find it!"

I blinked back the tears to focus on her. "What, Mom? Find what?"

"The book! You must find the book. It's in there."

A ripple of fear and excitement sliced through my beating heart.

Was she talking about the Book of the Order?

"Mom? What book? The Book of the Order of Witch

Hunters?" I watched her face as she slowly faded back to oblivion.

"The Book...Alexandra." She whispered. I crept closer to her face so I could hear. "Get the book. It's in there. The way...forward...is...in...there..."

With that, she drifted back into the solace of her curse, leaving the rest of us behind to wonder...

∽

THE WITCHY ADVENTURE CONTINUES WITH:

"Hexes and Hero's" Castle Point Witch Series Book 3
    Available Now!
    https://tammytyreebooks.com/collections/castle-point-witch-series-1

"Welcome back to the final installment in the enchanting world of Castle Point, where Alexandra now rules as the fierce Dagon Queen, calling the shots over her devoted squad of witch hunters.

But hold onto your broomsticks because Blake just stumbled upon a major revelation – his "dead" parents are alive and kicking, and they've been hiding from some seriously nasty enemies.

Family secrets, anyone?

Alex isn't one to back down from a challenge fueled by her sheer determination to crack the enigmatic code locked within the Book and reclaim her badass powers.

Against her better judgment, she can't resist helping Penny's cousin solve a bone—chilling demonic murder that's sending shivers through Castle Point.

As this epic tale unfolds, magic and love weave together, demanding some major sacrifices from Alex and her loyal coven. Together, they stand strong against the looming darkness threatening their whole world.

Along the way, they discover that love, family, and friendship are the true sources of power, uniting them in ways they never thought possible."

FOR READERS

Thank you for reading!

BONUS SCENE!!
    "Teddy's Terrible Time"
    https://dl.bookfunnel.com/9bg57njs7x
    For more books, please visit https://tammytyreebooks.com/

If you enjoyed this book, please leave a review on your favorite platform or on my website here: https://tammytyreebooks.com/products/castles----cauldrons

If you found spelling mistakes or niggly plot points, or you'd like to join my ARC/Beta Reader group please email the author directly: admin@tammytyree.com

Don't miss out on a single new release, discounts, and more!!

Sign up and we'll ensure you hear about every new book Tammy Tyree publishes as soon as it hits the stores.
    https://bit.ly/TyreeSubscribe

ALSO BY TAMMY TYREE

Fiction:

The Castle Point Witch Series

https://tammytyreebooks.com/collections/castle----point----
witch----series

Coming Soon:

The Corpse Collector Cozy Mystery Series

"Welcome to the "Corpse Collector Paranormal Women's Fiction
Cozy Mystery Series," starring Carrigan, a sassy 40-something
body removal expert. She's not just wrangling bodies at Castle
Point Funeral Home; she's also juggling chatty ghosts helping
crack the cases of their demises. With humor as her sidekick,
Carrigan unravels mysteries while keeping the afterlife laugh-out-
loud lively."

Non—Fiction

"Dead Men Still Snore: A Woman's True Story of Love, Loss, and
Channeling her Husband's Messages from the Other Side."

FOR AUTHORS

Are you an author, looking to up—level your career, your writing, or your time? The Author Revolution Academy has everything you need to succeed!**

Aspiring & Emerging Author Courses

Are you working toward getting your very first book out? Maybe you have a small (but growing backlist of titles)... If so, look no further. These courses are the best fit for you.

The Story Cure: http://bit.ly/410XVqW

Plan Your Series Challenge: http://bit.ly/3GFAv27

Indie Publishing Fundamentals: http://bit.ly/3GDrd6W

Prolific Author Course

Ready to take self—publishing to the next level? Rapid Release Roadmap is the course to get it done. Learn how to plan, write, publish, and promote 4 books (or more) every single year in this one—of—a—kind course!

Rapid Release Road Map: http://bit.ly/3o8b8zu

Millionaire Author Courses

Want to learn how to apply the Law of Attraction and manifestation techniques to your author career? Look no further! These courses (or membership) are just what you're looking for!

Millionaire Author Challenge: http://bit.ly/43osfNP

Millionaire Author Manifestation: http://bit.ly/3KoY5RQ

Abundant Author Activation: http://bit.ly/3MA2Iew

**Affiliate links

ABOUT THE AUTHOR

Tammy Tyree is a retired Board Certified Clinical Hypnotherapist and award-winning author of paranormal suspense and memoir.

Most of her professional career was dealing with entity attachments and demonic possession, which she thought was rather fun. Now, she works alongside International Best-selling author Carissa Andrews to up-level the lives of aspiring authors to manifest millionaire author careers.

She has four adult children and one incredibly perfect granddaughter whom she sees and spoils regularly.

You can follow Tammy on social or reach out to her via her website: www.tammytyreebooks.com

Book an "Inner Light Insight" Hypnotherapy / Psychic Session with Tammy! https://tammytyree.com

"Discover. Heal. Empower. Illuminate Your Path Within."

An Inner Light Insight session is a transformative 60-minute experience that blends the power of Hypnotherapy, Reiki, Energy Work, Tarot, Channeling, and more. This session will guide you on a holistic journey of self-discovery, healing, and empowerment.

Tammy is dedicated to helping you tap into your inner wisdom and unlock your full potential. Whether seeking personal growth, spiritual guidance, or a path to inner peace, our tailored sessions are thoughtfully crafted to illuminate the path to your true self.

Inner Light Insight

ILLUMINATE YOUR PATH WITHIN

www.ingramcontent.com/pod-product-compliance
Lightning Source LLC
Chambersburg PA
CBHW051242250626
47155CB00009B/3129